ig...

5 ribbons "What I thought would be a cute read turned into much more. J.W. McKenna has written a story that grabs your attention and doesn't let go until the last word. It has something for everyone: laughter, found love, suspense and a little sex thrown in. WANTED: KEPT WOMAN is definitely a keeper and worth a second read." ~ *Claudia McRay Romance Junkies*

4 stars "J. W. McKenna has once again created a beautiful and suspenseful world of erotic love.... This will be a HOT purchase for those who love subtle BDSM theme stories." ~ *Julie Esparza Just Erotic Romance Reviews*

4.5 stars "WANTED: KEPT WOMAN by J.W. McKenna is a sensuous romance with a touch of humor and a dash of danger that will keep you riveted to each hot page. You won't need your flannel jammies and hot cocoa to keep you warm as you read this scorcher, just sit back and enjoy!" ~ *Donna eCataRomance*

J.W. McKenna

WANTED: Kept Woman

Ellora's Cave
Romantica Publishing

An Ellora's Cave Romantica Publication

www.ellorascave.com

Wanted: Kept Woman

ISBN #1419951955

Edited by: Mary Moran
Cover art by: Syneca

Electronic book Publication: September, 2004
Trade paperback Publication: October, 2005

Warning:

The following material contains graphic sexual content meant for mature readers. *Wanted: Kept Woman* has been rated *S-ensuous* by a minimum of three independent reviewers.

Ellora's Cave Publishing offers three levels of Romantica™ reading entertainment: S (S-ensuous), E (E-rotic), and X (X-treme).

S-e*nsuous* love scenes are explicit and leave nothing to the imagination.

E-*rotic* love scenes are explicit, leave nothing to the imagination, and are high in volume per the overall word count. In addition, some E-rated titles might contain fantasy material that some readers find objectionable, such as bondage, submission, same sex encounters, forced seductions, etc. E-rated titles are the most graphic titles we carry; it is common, for instance, for an author to use words such as "fucking", "cock", "pussy", etc., within their work of literature.

X-*treme* titles differ from E-rated titles only in plot premise and storyline execution. Unlike E-rated titles, stories designated with the letter X tend to contain controversial subject matter not for the faint of heart.

Also by J.W. McKenna:

Darkest Hour

Lord of Avalon

Naughty Girl

Slave Planet

The Cameo

The Hunted

Wanted: Kept Woman

Chapter One

Brian Armstrong had had enough. *Maybe I'm just too old to fall in love anymore,* he mused. Even as he thought it, he scoffed. *Hell, I'm only forty. That's not exactly over the hill.*

It was Monday morning, ten o'clock. He looked down from his office on the thirtieth floor and reflected on his disappointing date last Saturday night. How could someone who appeared to be so attractive turn out to be so bull-headed? God, everything had to be her way!

Is it me? What am I doing wrong?

He turned and opened his coat closet. A full-length mirror showed him to be in pretty good shape for a middle-aged, desk-bound CEO. Tall, trim, with shoulders that could be called broad if one was being generous. Tailored suit, silk tie. Salt and pepper hair surrounded a reasonably handsome face, but then, he was hardly the one to judge.

He turned sideways, patting his stomach. Still flat—thanks to a hell of a lot of sit-ups at the gym. *So, what's the problem? I'm rich, I own my own company, I'm fit, some might even call me good-looking—why can't I find a woman who is a good fit? Someone who loves me for who I am and doesn't try to change me.*

He already knew the answer. Half the women he dated were blinded by his wealth. He could almost see the dollar signs in their eyes when they gazed upon him and hear their inner voices clamoring to be saved from a lifetime of drudgery. A rich man meant a big house, servants, shiny new cars. Cocktail parties every weekend. Hanging out with the upper crust. It didn't matter that Brian had no desire to be a social climber. Like most women, they probably figured they would change him after they snared him.

To that end, they would do anything to stay on his good side, becoming whoever he wanted them to be. Finding their true personalities was like digging for buried treasure. Often, after all that effort, their true selves were more like rhinestones than rubies.

The other half came from rich families already, so money wasn't the issue. However, their sense of entitlement usually spoiled them. When they went out with him, they were like thoroughbreds—nothing but the best would do. The finest restaurants, the poshest clubs, the most expensive vacations. They had to be seen by others of their class.

Hell, he thought, *I just don't have their pretensions. Sometimes I like to go bowling or eat fish and chips at a greasy diner.*

If he ever suggested such lowbrow entertainment to one of his upper-crust dates, the sneer in her eyes would tell him exactly what she thought of the idea. There'd be a hint of a curled lip, a narrowing of the eyes and she'd say, "You want to do *what*?" as if he'd lost his mind.

"Maybe I'm just a blue-collar guy in a white-collar world," he said aloud, and looked around to make sure he was still alone in his spacious office. It wouldn't do to be caught talking to himself. He stared at his reflection. "Or maybe I'm too particular."

But how would he know? He was too close to it. He needed an outside opinion. Brian thought of himself as a problem-solver. He'd successfully solved problems in his business, driving Armstrong Control Systems to become the third-largest supplier of computerized production control systems to manufacturers. He could conceivably retire today a wealthy man.

But so far I've been a miserable failure at love, he mused. *I'm tired of dating, trying to figure out if we're compatible. I'd like to cut through a lot of the wasted time. Why can't I apply the same techniques I learned in business to my desire to find a good woman?*

He closed the closet door and returned to his desk. He sat down, put his feet up and leaned back, fingers interlaced behind his neck. *Well,* he thought, *I could hire a dating service. Or try that "Speed Dating" I saw on the TV news once.*

But somehow, those seemed too generalized for him. He'd still have to go on endless dates to find that special woman. One he'd like to marry and have kids with. What he'd really like to do is eliminate all the gold-diggers and the sycophants. Tailor a solution for him alone. One that cut through the clutter, the wasted time.

He sat up suddenly and placed both feet on the ground. He reached across the clear expanse of desk and flipped the intercom.

"Yes?" The voice of his secretary Rebecca Detwiler came through.

"Would you come in here a minute, please?"

Three seconds later, the door opened. Rebecca had her dark blonde hair in a bun as usual. It fit her personality—efficient, competent and organized. Driven, like he was. That's why he'd hired her so many years ago when he had his choice of much younger and more attractive secretaries. But he hadn't wanted a looker, he had wanted someone who could be a teammate. Rebecca, now in her mid-fifties, would not have allowed any hanky-panky anyway. She'd been happily married for twenty-two years.

Now, when faced with the friendly but serious face of his secretary, Brian suddenly felt at a loss for words about his plans for his latest project. He could feel himself on the verge of embarrassment. He decided to ease into it.

"Come, sit down."

She strode to one of the two chairs in front of his desk and sat, smoothing the skirt of her business suit as she did. She held a notepad in her hands, a pen poised.

He waved his hands. "This is all off the record, okay?"

She appeared briefly puzzled then put the notepad into her lap, folding her hands over it. She merely waited, an expectant look on her face.

"Rebecca, how long have you been my secretary?"

"Eight years next month," she replied without hesitation.

"So you've gotten to know me pretty well, wouldn't you say?"

Rebecca's eyebrows twitched. "Yes, Brian, I have." Her boss had long ago forbidden her to call him "sir"—he had said it made him feel old. Besides, after eight years, they'd become friends.

"So, through the years, you're, um, familiar with my dating history." Brian could feel a red blush creep up his neck. He fought to stay focused. *This is just another problem to solve! No need to be embarrassed.*

Rebecca's right eyebrow went all the way up and she allowed a small grin to show. "Yes, to some extent. Of course, most of that takes place after business hours."

"About how many of the women that I've dated have you met?"

Rebecca thought for a moment. "Well, that's hard to say. You don't bring many of them around, except when they're meeting you for lunch." She stared over Brian's head for a moment. "I'd say maybe five or six."

"What did you think of them? I mean, generally?"

"Ooh, we are getting into rather dangerous territory, aren't we?" Her voice was light, but she spoke the truth. Brian could remember the time he'd been dating Nancy, a thoroughbred of the highest order. Rebecca had tried to warn him about her, after the woman had made some rude, off-hand comment about Brian while waiting for him outside his office. Brian had dismissed the warning abruptly, only later realizing Rebecca had been right—Nancy had been completely wrong for him.

"Yes, well," he struggled to regain his momentum. "I value your insight, Rebecca. You know that." He tugged at his tie. "I'm just taking stock. Um, if I asked you—out of those five or six that you met, how many would you say had been a good fit for me?"

"Oh, dear." She let her eyes fall to the floor for a moment then brought them up to Brian's face. "I didn't get to know them very well, but, uh, I'd have to say, none."

Brian just stared, wondering if his judgment in women was that far off or if Rebecca was being too harsh. "And why is that, do you think?"

"Do you really want to know?"

Brian knew what she meant—*Am I going to get in trouble if I speak my mind?*

He sighed. "I promise not to be churlish. I hope you know you can talk to me freely. Am I the kind of boss who only wants to hear good news?"

She smiled. Brian could see it light up her eyes. "No, you're always a very straightforward kind of guy." She stared at him and when he didn't say anything further, she plunged ahead. "I'd say it was because you're…dominant."

"What?"

"Dominant. Not just in love but in your business as well. Look at what you created here by sheer force of will." She waved a hand around his office and Brian knew she meant the entire company.

"Well, yeah, but that's different."

"I don't think so." She smiled and tipped her head. "I can't believe that this hasn't occurred to you."

"What? That I should treat women the same way I tackle business problems?"

"No, that there are women who really like…uh, a strong man."

"I thought they liked the sensitive type."

"Some do. And I think that's what you've tried to be, probably because of the way you've been brought up. Very respectful toward women." She paused. "I hope I'm not overstepping my bounds here."

Brian wanted to reassure her. He was fascinated by her ideas. "No, no. Please. I want to hear this." She was telling him what he'd been denying himself.

"It's just that there are some women who like to be…um, controlled, taken." Now it was her turn to blush. "Maybe it's the cavewoman in us. Maybe it's genetics. I don't know. All I'm saying is that I suspect you've been dating the wrong kind of women."

He leaned back, confused. "So you're saying I want…what? A little mouse?" That didn't seem right.

"No. You want a woman who is smart, sexy, good-looking—and submissive."

Brian sat all the way back, his mouth pursed as he thought that through. He knew what a submissive woman was, of course. He wasn't naïve. Secretly, he supposed he had been looking for a woman like that, although he had never put that label on it. He had simply hoped he might find a woman who wouldn't challenge him at every turn. Still…

"I'm not sure I want a doormat, Rebecca."

"Oh, you can have a submissive woman and not have her be a doormat. There are nuances. In fact, for many it's a game they play. Not all submissives do it twenty-four/seven."

"You seem to know a lot about this."

She blushed again. "Uh, well." She waved her hands.

Brian sat up. "Hey… You're telling me *you're* a submissive?"

"Not in the workplace," she responded at once. "But at home, John and I have been known to act out things on occasion."

Brian stared at her. He'd never known that side of her before. She seemed so accomplished, so professional. He didn't know exactly what went on behind closed doors at the Detwiler home, but he suspected that's why she had been so happily married for all these years.

"Does he tie you up and spank you or something?" He blurted the question before he could stop himself.

"I'm not telling." She smiled enigmatically. "That's between me and John."

"Uh, sorry. Didn't mean to pry." He paused. "Do you attribute the success of your marriage to this?"

"Yes, I'd have to say so."

Brian sat back again, and put his hands behind his head. He found himself strangely excited by the thought. "Wow… If that's the kind of woman I need, how can I go about finding her? What techniques must I apply?"

"Ahhh," she raised up a delicate finger to the ceiling, "because you're so successful, you think all of your problems can be solved by applying logic. As you've said so yourself many times, women aren't logical."

"Yeah, why is that, anyway? Why can't women be more logical?"

She flashed him an enigmatic smile. "Like Henry Higgins, 'Why can't a woman be more like a man', right?"

He laughed. "Okay. So I want to be in control, and I want to find a woman who…um, enjoys having a man who's in control." He rolled his eyes. "So what would you do, if you were me?"

"If I were you, I'd take out a personal ad."

He stared at her for a second and burst out laughing. "That's it? That's your idea?"

"Unless you have something better."

"Um, no, but it's not a very original idea."

"Well, that may be true. I mean, the ad by itself. I suggest you have a follow-up questionnaire that asks certain questions to determine how they view relationships. Then you could sort them out a little better."

Brian sat back in his chair. "Wow. You think they'd fill out a questionnaire like that?"

"A submissive woman probably would."

"Huh." Brian felt the thrill of the possibilities course through him. "What do you think the ad should say?"

"I think, for you, it should be straightforward, like your personality." She leaned forward. "I could help you with that, if you'd like."

Now it was his turn to smile. "I was hoping you'd say that." In his mind, he couldn't shake the image of Rebecca being spanked by her husband, whether it was true or not.

Chapter Two

Shortly after noon, Suzanne Montgomery drove to a mall just off San Francisco's Union Square and went inside to a small restaurant where she knew she'd be left alone. She wasn't in the mood to share her lunch hour with co-workers. Not today. She felt selfish and cranky.

Passing the entrance, she saw the latest issue of the local free tabloid. The blaring headline warned of skullduggery at City Hall but that didn't interest Suzanne. She liked to amuse herself by reading the Personals, much like someone who never takes vacations might like to read the travel section.

She sat at a table near the back, away from the other diners. The waitress took her order and left. Now Suzanne had a few glorious minutes to herself. She opened the paper and began reading, hoping, someday she might find a decent guy there in twenty-five words or less.

Yeah, right, she thought.

She was naturally suspicious of anyone who would take out an ad—even though she'd toyed with the idea herself a time or two. Of course, she wouldn't be like the lonely people she read about. She would be different. More refined, more desirable. But she never could bring herself to actually place the ad. Besides, she didn't know how to word it in a way that didn't make her sound desperate.

I'm only thirty-two, she told herself. *I'll find someone special. I'm neat, smart, pretty—Okay, so I've gained a few pounds since my horrible divorce, who hasn't? Where are all the good men? Why don't they ask me out?*

Twice, she actually answered ads, to her own surprise. The men had sounded intelligent and mysterious. Each time, she had imagined him to be tall, dark and handsome—although short, blond and ordinary would be okay as long as they weren't jerks—and they would be smitten by an earnest brunette with a winning smile and a shy but good-natured personality. The first time, she never heard back a peep. The second time, he called and they met for coffee. He hadn't exactly been what she looked for in a man—shorter than she expected and starting to go bald—but he had certainly been nice to her. It had seemed to go well, but he never called her again.

Was it something I said? Wasn't I thin enough for him?

Now she just read the Personals for fun, she had told her best friend Wendy.

"Oh, come on, Suzanne," she'd responded. "You gave it two tries since your divorce and you're ready to run for cover? Good God, woman, if you'd been Eisenhower during World War II, we'd all be speaking German today! Get real! You can't win the lottery if you don't buy a ticket!"

Easy for her to say, Suzanne thought. Wendy Thomason never wanted for dates. She was tall and slender, and good-looking. She had long blonde hair that she often kept in a bun that most men itched to unravel. Twice when they were walking down the street together, Suzanne had seen men walk into poles, their eyes riveted by this Nordic goddess.

Sometimes Suzanne wondered why she hung around with Wendy. Just looking at her made her depressed. She felt like such a frump in comparison. But they'd been friends since high school. She knew Wendy had a good heart and really cared about her. In fact, Wendy would be disappointed that Suzanne thought herself frumpy. "You're a good-looking woman, Suze," she'd tell her. "You just need to quit wearing your sadness on your face."

Today, as she ate her cheeseburger and scanned the paper, she wasn't looking for anything in particular. She was just passing time. That's when the small personal ad caught Suzanne's attention: "Wanted: Kept woman for wealthy businessman. Call…"

She stared at the words, shocked. Questions ran into each other in Suzanne's mind. Can you advertise for something like that? What is a kept woman anyway? Does he want a beautiful gold-digger, good for nothing but fucking and shopping? She giggled at the idea.

Ha! What a life that would be! For a moment, she could imagine herself, stretched out in a king-sized bed, nicely satiated after a good morning fuck. Her keeper or sugar daddy or whatever you call him would smile, touch her cheek and wink, and head off to work, leaving her with the rest of the day to lie about the pool or to go shopping.

Wow. Not bad, she thought.

She laughed and stuck the paper into her purse, mentally dismissing the ad, although the fantasy lingered. *Why is that?* she wondered. After all, Suzanne had sought the protection of a strong man before, and it hadn't exactly worked out as promised. Absently, she rubbed the side of her face, as if she could still feel the bruise.

Sighing, she looked at her watch and knew it was time to head back. Her body ached at the thought. Working for a catalogue fulfillment warehouse the week before school starts can do that to you, she reflected. All the kids wanted their new school clothes *right now*. And for some reason, the fashions offered by the Blue Bayou Co. were all the rage this year.

Blue Bayou. Suzanne shook her head at the name. The closest this company had been to the bayou was when her boss, Jack Smyth, flew over Louisiana in a jet. He just plucked the name out of thin air, thinking it sounded "cool". When she had signed on two years ago, the job was just going to be temporary. Now, at age thirty-two, she felt trapped by it.

She should never have taken that promotion! Moving from the warehouse floor into the office had promised to be easier, but it simply added a new layer of duties to her schedule. During busy times, she still was expected to "help out" on the floor when the staff fell behind on their orders. Trouble was, they were so short-staffed Suzanne had to fill in quite a bit. Meanwhile, her paperwork piled up on her desk, forcing her to work extra hours to catch up.

She left the mall and slid into her car. She glanced at her makeup in the rearview mirror. Suzanne frowned at the puffiness that had crept into her face over the last few years. Still, her friends reassured her how pretty she was. She had an oval face with wide-set amber eyes, surrounded by a well-kept halo of brown hair. Mike, the handsome married man in shipping, even told her one day that she looked a lot like actress Sigourney Weaver, "only shorter". Suzanne had immediately thought, *and fatter*.

"You're always putting yourself down," Wendy had told her on many occasions.

She knew her friend was right. She tried to be positive, but her life seemed like such a mess right now.

"I need a new life," she told her reflection. "Can I do a trade-in?"

*****

That evening, on her couch in her tiny apartment, sharing a bottle of wine, she listened as Wendy told her how miserable *her* life had become. Suzanne wanted to smother her with a pillow.

"I'm telling you, Suze, the men I'm meeting lately are crass and crude. No style. No taste. They just want to fuck me and if I say no, they just shrug and move on, like if I won't, they'll find someone who will—and they probably do. What's wrong with guys nowadays?"

Suzanne didn't know—she couldn't remember the last time *she'd* been laid. And her vibrator didn't count. "Maybe you should just let them," she said without thinking.

A brief smile stole across Wendy's face. "Well, yeah, if they're worthy." It was followed immediately by a grimace. "But so many aren't—they're Peter Pans or self-centered assholes."

"At least you're getting laid when you want to!" she responded just a little too sharply.

Wendy looked up to see the pain on her friend's face. "I'm sorry, Suze. I'm just venting. I'm not trying to make you feel bad."

"No, it's all right," she said, a little embarrassed. "I'm a little envious, as you can tell. I don't get asked out much. Not since, you know..."

"You aren't missing much. I get invitations—it's just that most are from real jerks."

"Come on, they can't be as bad as Sam."

Wendy shrugged. "Well, no. Close, maybe." She paused, nibbling at her lower lip. "You know, you gotta stop comparing everyone to Sam. He was, um, unique. The odds that you'll run into another like him are very small."

"I know. I think I'm ready to really get out there and try again. I'm certainly interested. I'm...I'm just scared. When I met Sam, I thought he was 'The One'." She made quote marks in the air.

Wendy held out her hands, palms up, like an imaginary scale. "So, let's see... You've got your fear of meeting another Sam versus your—what?—horniness quotient?" She moved her hands up and down as if finding a balance.

Suzanne giggled. "Um, yeah, that's it. Only, I think horniness is starting to edge ahead."

"That's the spirit! Like an ancient Chinese philosopher once said," she faked a Charlie Chan accent, showing her front teeth, "You don't haffa find Mr. Right. You only haffa find Mr. Long." Wendy winked at her.

Suzanne guffawed and put her hand up over her mouth in mock horror. "So you're saying, I should just get laid and forget trying to find Mr. Right?!" She stopped short of adding, "like you do."

"No, I'm not saying you should fuck the first guy that comes along." Wendy frowned. "Wait, maybe I am. You need to get laid just to clear your head. Get the cobwebs out. Then you can start looking more carefully. That's what I'd do. You never know who might turn up, a gem among the Jimmies."

"A sweetheart among the swine."

"A cock among the cockroaches!"

"A tool among the fools!" Suzanne giggled.

"That's it! So what if you screw a few men who aren't perfect? You'll be gaining some needed experience for when Mr. Right comes along."

Just listening to Wendy talk about men made her realize how long it had been. *God, I am horny!* She squeezed her legs together. "Okay, tell me about the last time you made love. What was he like? What happened?"

Wendy eyed her friend speculatively. Suzanne knew what she was thinking. Whenever Suzanne felt particularly depressed, she liked to listen to Wendy's descriptions of her recent liaisons. She wanted them as graphic as possible—even if Wendy had to embellish.

"Are you sure?" Wendy shot her a sly smile.

"Yes! I'm sure. You know I love your stories. If I can't have a man of my own, at least I can share one of yours."

"Okay, as long as you promise to try." She looked meaningfully at Suzanne until she nodded. "Let's see. That would be Jerry…"

"Wait! Let me, um, change position." Suzanne moved her upholstered chair around until her back was toward Wendy. "Okay. Go ahead." This was their little game—they both enjoyed it but neither one wanted to watch the other during the next few minutes.

"Okay. Jerry," Wendy continued. "I think you met him once, he's tall, brown hair, broad-shouldered—the construction worker?"

"Yeah," Suzanne said dreamily. "I remember."

"Anyway, he's kinda self-centered—"

"No! Don't ruin it! Just the fucking, tell me about the fucking!"

"Oh. Okay. We went to that new place for dinner—Nelson's on 3rd, near the waterfront? I had the prime rib."

"Wen!"

"Oh, sorry. I was just working up to it. Let's see. He took me home and I invited him in…"

"Now you're talking."

"He kissed me, hard, just as soon as we entered. God, that man is so strong, he could break me in half! He has biceps the size of footballs. For a minute, I wanted to push him off, to be the coy little tease, just to keep him honest don'tcha know. It was our first date and all. But then he reached down and picked me up like I didn't weigh anything, all the while kissing me and I just about came right there."

"Oh, man, Wen, I'm getting horny just thinking about it." Suzanne tugged at her jeans, which suddenly were beginning to ride up on her.

"Anyway, he carried me into my bedroom. I hadn't even made the bed! I was so embarrassed—"

Suzanne shook her head. "You're losing your audience!"

"Sorry. So, he practically drops me on the bed and begins to strip off his clothes. See, normally, it's the other way around, the man strips you naked while he's fully dressed. But this way, it was like he was the vulnerable one. Yeah, as if! So, I'm lying there in my black cocktail dress—my shoes still on—and he's doing a slow striptease. Oh, man, I wish I had it on videotape!"

Suzanne closed her eyes and visualized it as Wendy kept up the narration. Without even being aware of it, Suzanne's hand crept down to the front of her jeans and unsnapped the catch.

"So off comes the shirt, then the shoes and pants, all nice and slow. He wears boxer shorts and it looked like the circus was in town, if ya know what I mean."

Oh, yes, Suzanne could visualize Jerry's erection, pressing hard against the cotton material as if it were a tent. Maybe there'd be just a little wet stain of pre-cum at the tip.

"So he hooks both thumbs under the elastic and slowly, ever so slowly, drags them down. My god, when his cock came out, I swore I could hear strains of the soundtrack from '2001' in my head. It was *big*."

Suzanne was rhythmically squeezing her thighs together, her face blank, eyes still closed. Her hand pressed hard against her mound. Wendy's story and her own imagination worked very well together.

"Now he's naked and I'm still dressed. Any thoughts that maybe I wasn't in the mood have gone right out the window. If Jerry had tried to leave at that moment, I'm telling you, I'd have jumped *him*.

"So he comes over close to me, so close I can smell the Old Spice he wears and unclasps my pearls. You know the ones I bought while I was shopping at that new place on."

"Wendy, if you get sidetracked one more time, I swear I'm going to go play with my vibrator!" She pulled her hand away from between her legs in exasperation and waited for Wendy to continue.

"Oh, yeah. Sorry. He reaches down and gently rolls me on my side so he can get to my zipper. It goes all the way down to my ass. I can hear him unzip it slowly as if he has all the time in the world. He sits me up. I'm very pliable at this point, don't cha know. He pulls me to my feet and lets the dress just fall away. Then he eases me back down. I'm just wearing my garter belt and stockings, black bra and panties."

Wendy, eyes closed, recalling the evening, let her hand move to the front of her dress. Her legs fell open.

"He gets down on his knees and pushes my legs apart. My panties, as you can imagine, are soaked by now. I'm having trouble catching my breath." Like Suzanne, she pressed her hand against her mound.

"He reaches around behind me and unhooks my bra. Oh, my breasts ached when they were freed! He gently rubs a nipple with his thumb and it stood straight out. He does the same to the other one. I could feel it all the way down into my privates… Hang on, I have to, um, make an adjustment."

"Yeah, me too," Suzanne breathed and brought her hand back to her groin. She unzipped her jeans to give herself more room. She pressed three fingers hard against her clit through her panties but the jeans were still in the way. She wished she had on a dress right now, like Wendy.

"Jerry unsnaps the stockings and rolls them down my legs one at a time. I have to lean back on my elbows and raise my legs for him and I'm sure he can see how wet I am. But I don't feel awkward at all."

Suzanne pressed her hand to her clit again and felt sparks shoot up through her stomach. She imagined Wendy was doing the same thing and it somehow excited her. After all, they were very good friends, even though both were strictly straight.

"Now you know I like to shave down there. And Jerry hadn't seen me naked yet. I mean, all of me. So when he goes for my panties, I'm watching his face to see his reaction, you know. I have to lean way back and raise my hips a little."

"Oh, shit, Wen, my pants are too tight."

"That's okay," she said. Suzanne could hear her friend fumbling with her own clothes.

Suzanne pushed her unzipped jeans down to the tops of her thighs and cupped her mound. It was burning up.

"God, I'm so hot. Go on."

"Right. So, he pulls down my black bikini panties and as my pussy is exposed, he whistles! Kinda soft and low. He says it's beautiful. Then he leans in. I can see the tip of his tongue come out. Oh, my god, Suze, he likes oral! I thought I'd died and gone to heaven. He just touches the tip of his tongue to my clit and I swear to god, I came immediately. Just like that. I thought the top of my head would explode."

Suzanne stroked herself with two fingers, feeling the wetness soak through her panties. She could hear Wendy follow suit, the soft squishing of their pussies obvious. Each pretended not to notice the other. That was part of their game.

"He pulls my panties off completely. I'm a cooked noodle now. My pussy's so wet I'm making a big puddle on the bed. His cock is like a five-cell flashlight and my cave needed some illumination, don't cha know. So I'm expecting the big push, you know, and I'm all ready for it. But he surprises me. He climbs over me and rests his big hard cock against my thigh, teasing me, about an inch away from you-know-what. Then he leans down and starts sucking my nipple."

"Oh, god, Wen—which one?" She rubbed herself harder now. The sheer panties seemed too thick, so she slipped her hands under the waistband and let her fingers dive into her slit. She quickly found her hidden pearl and rubbed, slowing it down a little bit to keep pace with Wendy's story.

"The left one. He sucks it and I came again—just a little one. Like a pre-shock before the big quake. He sucks the other one and I think I might come again the same way. I'm telling you, Suze, I could feel my pussy waving now, trying to reach out for his cock, which is still against my thigh—and hard as a rock. I'm through being the demure first date. I reach down and grab that monster, and try to pull him up to me.

"But he's being coy, the bastard. He continues to kiss my nipples, even the sides of my throat, my ears—you know how I love that—and keeps his cock just out of reach. I mean, he's like a half-inch away and I'm pulling at it and trying to scrunch down—anything to get that man's cock in me, you know?"

Suzanne, eyes tightly closed, could picture it all right only she was the one on the bed, not Wendy, trying to pull this monster cock to her aching cunt. She was going to come soon now, very soon.

"So I'm starting to get vocal. I'm starting to cuss and say things like, 'Fuck me, fuck me, fuck me.' I'm stroking his cock now too. I love the way my hand feels on it. I can barely get my fingers around it.

"He lets me pull him toward me. He kisses me, softly, not like you'd expect from a big macho guy like Jerry. He kinda nibbles at my lower lip—I just love that! Meanwhile, my mind is elsewhere, ya know. The head of his cock is just parting my lips. I'm so wet now it's almost embarrassing. Almost." Her eyes are closed tightly, playing the scene out in her head, her fingers working steadily.

"Suddenly, and I'm telling you I was caught by surprise, he thrusts it right up into me a ways. My pussy was wide open and grabbing at him. I let go and he shoved that tool right up inside me."

Suzanne groaned aloud and bit her lip as she came hard. Her fingers held her throbbing clit tightly as the orgasm rocked her. Flashes of light sparkled the inside of her eyelids. Dimly, she was aware of the wet sound Wendy made, stroking her own clit. Her speech began to slow as she concentrated on her own orgasm.

"I came so hard I thought…I was going to die right there. It was…amazing. And he didn't stop… He kept pounding into me, pounding, pounding… I came again…and again. Then he thrust hard and…I could feel his cock spurting into me, gallons it felt like… I can't tell you how that made me feel, to have him so deep inside, coming and coming and…oh God… I'm cooomming!"

Wendy shuddered and grabbed herself tightly. For several long minutes, the two women sat there, facing away from each other, basking in the glow of their orgasms. Finally, Wendy sat up and adjusted her clothing. Suzanne pulled up her pants and zipped them. She stood and moved her chair back into position. They looked at each other, smiling.

"And that was my date with Jerry," Wendy said quietly, her body limp with relief.

Suzanne grinned. "Thanks for sharing. I feel much better now."

"Good. Now if you'll excuse me…" She disappeared into the guest bathroom. Suzanne went to her private bath to clean up as well.

"Are we still seeing Jerry?" she said a few minutes later when they had resettled themselves on the couch. Suzanne felt a small ownership of him now.

"Well, yes, off and on. Mostly off. As I said, he's rather self-centered. I think he loves himself more than he could ever love a woman. That doesn't work for me." She batted her eyes at Suzanne. "But, I keep him handy just for the occasional sex."

They laughed together. Modern women enjoying their sexuality, just like men.

"That's too bad, Jerry sounds like a keeper, conceited or not. Maybe you could send him my way when you're not using him. I don't think my standards are quite as high."

"Hey, I don't ask much—I just want a man who's sensitive, caring, well-hung, strong, generous, sexy, funny, intelligent…"

"Sounds like an ad in the personals," Suzanne teased.

"I'm not above that! I've met some nice guys there. Well, a few anyway. Hell, that's why I've encouraged you to try it—god knows you're not going to meet anyone in the warehouse."

"Oh, that reminds me, I found the oddest ad today in the *Bayside Weekly*! Here, I've still got it."

Suzanne fished the tabloid out of her purse and folded it to the right page. "Here. *'Wanted: Kept woman…'* Isn't that strange?"

Wendy scanned the ad. "Oh, boy, he'll get thousands of responses, don't cha think? Women love the rich."

"Or just a pervert, trying to lure in gullible women."

"I don't know. You'll never know unless you call."

Suzanne was shocked. "I'm not going to call! I'm not that desperate!" But she was thinking to herself, *He'd never want me – he's looking for someone like Wendy.*

"Why do you say that? Come on, this is me you're talking to! You've told me many times you'd marry for money! Maybe this is some rich old guy like that guy who married Anna Nicole Smith, you know? She ended up with forty million or something. You should at least call and find out more."

"I'm not answering that ad. I'm sure he's a troll. He probably looks like Steve Buscemi, you know, the actor with all the crooked teeth?"

"You always expect the worst! What could it hurt to find out?"

Wendy was right, Suzanne knew. She didn't really think he'd be ugly. She feared he would turn out to be like Sam.

The irony, she thought, *is that I liked the way Sam took charge.*

At first, anyway. He had strength and a certain amount of aggressiveness that she mistook for ambition. She had wanted to feel protected, let the man make the hard decisions. But Sam was a slave to his own jealousies. What started out as an ideal relationship in her mind quickly degenerated into anger, recriminations and abuse.

It had been more than two years since their ugly breakup, made worse when Sam wouldn't leave her alone. Even after the divorce, he'd hung around, scaring off other men and acting possessively toward her. Late last year, he violated a restraining order and slashed the tires on her car. She had caught him at it. She ran out to the parking lot, yelling at him and he'd reacted, punching her, cracking the orbit of her eye socket and giving her a black eye. She'd had him arrested. The judge gave him nine months in county jail. *Serves you right,* asshole.

The experience caused her to retreat into her shell, putting on some weight to hide herself from men. It didn't solve her problem, of course—she ached with loneliness. She wanted to date again. She needed a man—just not one like Sam.

"Come on, don't be a wuss."

"He doesn't want me," Suzanne said stubbornly.

"How do you know?"

"Because I'm too…too—you know!" she wailed, waving a hand up and down her body.

Wendy looked at her, shocked. "Now, Suzanne, I've known you all my life and I'm telling you, you look great. Okay, maybe you're carrying a couple extra pounds…"

"Oh, come on! I'm chubby!"

"No, you're not—you're a beautiful woman! You've got style and grace and a great sense of humor—"

"Oh, yeah, all the hallmarks of a fat chick. 'She has a great personality'," she mimicked in a high voice.

"You're not fat!" Wendy sat back, shoulders slumping.

Suzanne bit her lip. "Wen, let's face it—if I'm not fat, what am I? 'Pleasingly plump'?"

Wendy shook her head. "Well, I disagree…but if you feel that way, why don't you do something about it?"

She had her there. Suzanne had to admit she'd given up on herself. It was too easy to just go to work and come home and not think about trying to be attractive anymore. She could put on some different makeup and lose the weight if she wanted to. If she had a reason to.

"I know, I know. I've read all the articles—I use the weight as a defense mechanism to keep men away from me."

"Yes, you do. But you tell me all the time how lonely you are."

"I know. It doesn't make a lot of sense." Suzanne was feeling a little guilty about the cheeseburger she'd had for lunch. "That's why I could never answer an ad like that—I'd just be setting myself up for a big disappointment."

"You don't know that."

"I feel it in my bones, Wen."

"Okay, that's it." She stood and went to the phone.

"What are you doing?"

"I'm calling my hairdresser. A new 'do is the first step toward a new you!"

Chapter Three

Sam Carlucci stalked out of his cell at the Santa Clara County Jail, shoulders back. His dark hair was combed back and peaked in the center, like a refugee from the fifties. His face was hard, unsmiling, as if he'd been incarcerated for ten years, not seven months. He imagined himself a tough con, being led out of the Big House—hardened, mean and full of wicked new ideas. He carried his meager belongings in front of him in a small box—pictures, writings and toiletries. The beefy black deputy followed, tapping his nightstick lightly against his leg.

"Gonna be a good boy now, Sammy?" the guard asked, his voice rich with sarcasm.

"Yessuh, masta'," Sam replied. "Isa be a good boy now."

The deputy scoffed. "You sure talk funny for a white boy." He signaled the guard at the gate and stood back as the heavy metal grate slid to the side. Entering, the two men waited for it to close behind them, then another gate opened in front, allowing them to pass.

"This way," the guard said, though it was unnecessary—every inmate knew the way out. They walked down the cement corridor to a steel door with inch-high letters that said "Processing". The guard tapped on it with his stick and offered a final piece of advice to the sullen inmate.

"You know if ya screw up, you won't be comin' back to county—they'll send you' ass right to the big house, ya hear?"

Sam just nodded, his eyes flat, his anger kept in check. The door opened and he stepped through, almost into the arms of a massive black guard with biceps the size of loaves of bread that strained against his short-sleeved shirt. The guard moved aside. The room was small. At one end, stood a waist-high counter, topped by a wire mesh screen with a slot in the center. A skinny corrections officer sat on a stool, looking bored. The huge black man moved back to stand against the wall, near the only other door to the room, marked "Exit". He stared at Sam, as if daring him to do something stupid.

"Carlucci?" asked the officer behind the screen. Sam turned and nodded. The officer read from a clipboard. "Sam Carlucci, you are hereby being released by the County of Santa Clara for the crimes of assault and battery, stalking and malicious mischief. You've served seven months of a nine-month sentence and are being released under the stipulation that you are to have no contact with your ex-wife, Suzanne Montgomery. You are being notified that the restraining order is still in effect and that if you violate this order, you will be immediately returned to jail or other correctional facility and may face additional time. You must report to a probation officer regularly for a period of three years from today and you must submit to drug tests on a regular basis. Do you understand the terms of your release?"

Sam nodded again, keeping his anger in check. The guard shook his head. "You have to state your response out loud." He pointed to the video camera, aimed at Sam's face.

"I understand the conditions. I'm to have no contact with my ex-wife. I have to report to a probation officer."

Nodding, the guard walked farther back into a small storage area, out of sight.

"Take off your clothes," growled the large black officer behind him. Sam put down his box on the counter and began removing the blue jail smock, glad to be free of the hated outfit. While he was busy, the first officer returned and shoved a tray through the slot at the bottom of the screen.

"Sign for these," he said. Sam, naked now, approached the screen. He looked inside, spotting the clothes he'd come in here with. With much satisfaction, he began to put them on. Blue dress shirt, tan pants. He took the tie and tossed it into the trashcan. Brown socks and loafers completed the ensemble. The shoes pinched.

He felt like a new man. Or, at least a sense, that his life was returning to normal. Sam flexed his muscles under the shirt, surprised to discover that it fit tightly across the shoulders now. Lifting weights had done some good. He patted his stomach, feeling the ripple of his abs underneath the shirt.

Hey, lookin' good, he mused. *Santa Clara County's bodybuilding regimen seems to have paid off. Seven months to a new you!*

Sam opened the manila envelope in the bottom of the tray and took out his wallet, watch and his wedding ring. He counted his money—seventeen dollars. At least he hadn't been robbed by the guards. He held up the gold ring and let it catch the light. He was tempted to toss it into the trash with the tie but decided against it. He tucked it into his pants pocket instead.

"Sign here," the guard said.

Sam signed, not even reading what he was signing. *Fuck 'em.*

"This way," the massive guard said with a toss of his head, unlocking the other door with a key the size of a roll of nickels.

Sam didn't have to be told twice. He picked up his cardboard box and stepped through the opened door. The light seemed brighter here, the air fresher. He could see two long rows of glass blocks embedded into the cement wall across the hall. A beautiful late-summer sun illuminated them, casting a yellow-gold light into his eyes. He was almost out—he could taste it. Another guard waited for him, a skinny old guy everyone called Barney because he bore a passing resemblance to Barney Fife, the TV deputy.

"This way," the guard said. "You couldn'tna picked a better day to get out. Must be eighty-five degrees out there." They walked together down the corridor. Ahead, Sam could see the main door to the county jail. The last steel gate slid aside and he stepped through into the lobby. Barney accompanied him to the double glass doors.

"You take care of yourself now. We don't want to see you come back." He held open one of the doors for Sam.

"Oh, I won't," Sam said, and walked out, a free man.

"Bus stop's right there," Barney said, leaning out the open door, pointing. "Bus'll be along in about fifteen minutes."

Nodding, Sam turned toward the bench. He closed his eyes against the light because it hurt his eyes and walked blindly for a few steps, feeling the air, the sun and the wind as if for the first time.

When he reached the bench, he sat down, wishing he had a cigarette. He breathed deeply, filling his lungs with rich, free air.

Looking down into the box on his lap, he could see a dated snapshot of his ex-wife Suzanne smiling up at him.

He smiled back. "Bitch," he said.

Chapter Four

A week later, Suzanne had to admit that Wendy had been right. She'd started a diet and had already lost five pounds. Yesterday, Wendy had taken her down to get a new hairstyle—shorter and lighter, with highlights mixed in. She looked better, she felt better—wow! Even a small change can do wonders for one's self-image, she decided.

"See? I told you," Wendy told her as they met at the mall to celebrate her new look. Since Suzanne was skipping lunches, they had a full hour to check out some flattering dresses to show off her more slender body.

The women flew from store to store, trying on outfits and shoes and giggling like high school kids. Suzanne bought a new dress, plus a skirt and a pair of shoes. She used up her clothing allowance for the next six months.

"Don't worry about it," Wendy had told her. "When you meet your sugar daddy, this won't matter."

"Oh, yeah, right," she retorted. But she did feel more attractive now. The small changes had helped break her out of the doldrums.

"Here, the new issue's out," Wendy said suddenly, grabbing a free *Bayside Weekly* off the rack. "Let's find you a man, okay?"

Suzanne blushed and looked around. "Come on, Wen. Not so loud. You make me sound desperate!"

Wendy looked up from the paper. "Oh, sorry." She grinned. "But we can't let another day pass without sharing your new look with a brand-new man!"

"I'm an independent woman, I don't need..." she started to mutter, but Wendy had already walked away. She followed. They sat down on a bench, their heads together as they read the ads.

"Here's one, *'SWPM ISO fun-loving, smart, athletic SWF ages 26-36. NS preferred'*."

"Nah, 'athletic' means he doesn't want anyone who's..." Suzanne didn't want to say the "F" word as she no longer thought of herself that way. Yes, five pounds made that much difference. "...not really skinny."

"Oh, I don't know about that. You look great. Okay, try this one, *'SWDM seeks SWF for fun, walks in the park, movies, games and possible LTR. Must like kids'*." She paused. "Uh-oh."

Wendy put the down the paper and both women looked at each other. Simultaneously, they shrieked, "He wants a mom!"

"Yeah," Suzanne gasped. "He probably has four rotten kids and sole custody!"

"Can you imagine who'd respond to that ad? She'd be a woman with three rotten kids whose husband just ran off!"

They laughed and slapped their thighs. Other shoppers looked at them as if they were crazy women.

"Okay," Wendy said, tears in her eyes from laughter, "I'm willing to concede maybe that's not a good one!"

She began reading again. Suzanne was ready to chuck the paper in the trash and head back to work. It was amusing to read them, sure, but to actually answer—

"Hey!"

Wendy looked up from the paper. "Here's that ad again. The one you were talking about last week." She showed Suzanne the paper.

Wanted: Kept woman…

"Wow! Two weeks in a row! He must be really desperate!"

"Or maybe he just signed up for two weeks originally, not knowing how many responses he'd get. You never know," Wendy pointed out.

"Yeah, well, he probably looks like a toad. Or he's a perv."

"Well, I'm going to call to find out." Wendy fished her cell phone out of her purse.

Suzanne gasped. "No! You can't!" She started to rise. Wendy caught her arm and pulled her back down, then punched in some numbers. Suzanne tried to get away, but Wendy grabbed her arm again and held it.

"Hello? I'm calling about the ad? Uh-uh." She listened as Suzanne sat there, eyes wide.

"Yes, I can do that. Okay, here's the email address…"

Suzanne was stunned to hear Wendy give out Suzanne's email address. "You—!"

"Shh!" she said quickly, her hand over the mouthpiece. To the phone she said, "No, someone was talking. It's all right."

Wendy made a few more agreeable comments and hung up. She smiled at Suzanne.

"Well? What? What'd they say?"

"Oh, now you're curious? You, the girl who'd never answer another personal ad?"

Suzanne brought her hands up and made choking gestures in midair.

"Okay, okay," Wendy laughed. "She was very nice…"

"She?"

"She was the secretary. Or personal assistant. I'm not sure. Rebecca something. I'm telling you, Suze, this guy does sound rich."

"Why don't you date him then?"

Wendy put her hand over her heart. "Because I'm doing this for you. I know you'd never do this for yourself. You need a push and I'm pushing. Look at you. In a week you've lost some weight, gotten a whole new look and I'll bet you're feeling much better about yourself, right?"

Suzanne had to agree.

"So think of this as the next step in making the New Suzanne."

"I don't want to date this stranger! You're the one complaining about men lately! Why not go after him yourself?"

"Well, I could. We both could."

"What do you mean? A threesome?"

Wendy laughed. "God, no. I love ya, dear, but not like that! No, the secretary said we have to fill out a short questionnaire and send in a photo in order to get to the next step."

"Oh, right. I'll be sure and do that!" She'd already dismissed the idea as dangerous and stupid.

"Oh, no you don't," Wendy said. "I'm going to make sure you fill it out. And if you won't send in a photo, I'm sure I can find one in my collection somewhere…" She paused and looked toward the ceiling. "I can think of a time when you got drunk in Santa Barbara…"

"You wouldn't!"

"I would. Look, girlfriend, I'm going to bust you out of your rut if it's the last thing I do, okay? You don't have to marry the guy or even date him more than once, but you gotta get out there and try, you know?"

Suzanne nodded, secretly pleased that Wendy was pushing her into this. She would be far too shy to promote herself. Despite her grave misgivings, she thought she'd humor her friend and let her do this for her. It wouldn't go any further than this first step.

"Okay, but only if you fill it out on yourself as well."

Wendy shrugged. "What the hell. It could be fun. If it will make you do it, I'll do it too."

Chapter Five

The questionnaire sent to Suzanne by Rebecca the following day was simple and straightforward—at first. Age, height, weight, hair color, eye color, education, employment, likes and dislikes—just the facts, ma'am. On page two, however, the questions took a sudden sharp turn.

Do you have a sexual fantasy? Describe it.

How many lovers have you had?

Do you enjoy sex?

Have you ever engaged in sex games? What kind?

What's your idea of a "kept" woman?

Suzanne gasped and called up Wendy. "Get your ass over here! You won't believe this!"

Wendy showed up within minutes, breathless with excitement. Suzanne poured them each a glass of wine. "Where? Show me!" Without a word, Suzanne handed her a glass and a printout of the invasive questions.

"Oh my god! This is great!" Wendy squealed. She took a big sip while reading.

"Great? This is sick. No way I'm answering that! This is just some guy getting his jollies. That 'secretary' is probably some horny teenager's cousin or sister." The cautionary Suzanne was speaking now, she realized. A deeper part of her shivered with excitement.

"Oh, no, she didn't sound like that. She seemed very professional. But you should call her yourself. Look, there's a phone number at the bottom."

"No, dammit. The fun's over. I'm not about to tell my secrets to someone I don't even know. Hell, I don't even tell my boyfriends stuff like this until we've gone out six months at least." Suzanne found herself saying the words, yet hoping Wendy would talk her into taking the next step.

"If you call, maybe she'll tell you more about this man."

"No, no! I'm too scared."

"Oh, come on! Don't be such a baby. Wouldn't you rather answer some questions now and get the right guy for you than show up for a blind date and be paired with some troll?"

"There's no guarantee he isn't a troll anyway."

Wendy shook her head. "I don't think so. I get the feeling he's on the level."

"What brings you to that conclusion?"

"Just the whole way he's going about this—having his secretary set things up, the questionnaire. He's trying to narrow down the list. This guy has 'Donald Trump' written all over him."

"Oh, god! I don't want to date Donald Trump!"

"You know what I mean. You should at least take the first step."

Suzanne allowed herself to consider the idea. "You really think so? You don't think he's a stalker?"

"No, I don't. And you know how I can read men."

Suzanne's conservative side jumped in again. "Oh, yeah—like Archie last year? That was a great read."

Wendy made a face. "One slip-up and you never let me live it down. How was I to know he was on probation?"

"Yeah, for flashing!"

Wendy held up a hand, her wineglass steady in the other. "All right, all right. But you know, overall, I'm a pretty good judge of men."

Suzanne shrugged. "Yeah. You did try to warn me about Sam."

Wendy rolled her eyes. "Yeah. At least I didn't *marry* any of my mistakes!"

Suzanne took a healthy drink of wine. Her face showed she was thinking about it. Wendy jumped on it.

"Come on. I will if you will."

Suzanne took the paper from her friend and read through it. She bit her bottom lip. Could she really do this? Then she spotted something at the bottom of the page.

"Oh, no!"

"What?"

"They want two photos, a head shot and a full-body shot!"

"Clothed?" Wendy put in.

Suzanne shot her a level look. "You slut. Come on, Wendy, that's going to kick me right out of the running. I'm still too f— Well, not skinny enough yet. I can't do this."

"You are *not* fat! You're not even pleasingly plump anymore. Besides, maybe he likes a woman with a little padding. Maybe he's looking for a good breeder—you never know!"

Suzanne gasped. "No! Stop that! Now I'm sure I don't want to do this. This is the craziest idea you've ever come up with."

"Oh, come on. I'm going to do it. I brought my digital camera. This will be fun. We'll get a little drunk, and send them in and forget about it, okay?"

By herself, Suzanne never would have taken such a dramatic step. Yet, the support of her friend emboldened her. She allowed her reckless side to push aside her conservative side for once in her life. She gave Wendy a half-grin. *Come on*, she told herself, *what could be the harm?*

"Okay." She sighed elaborately. "I'll just consider it practice, a way to get my nerve up for meeting a real man. Now pour me another glass of wine."

They each filled out their questionnaires carefully, trying not to exaggerate too much. "The woman on the phone stressed that honesty was of critical importance," Wendy told her.

"Maybe so, but I'm subtracting another five pounds because I fully intend to lose it," Suzanne retorted.

Let's see, age: 32; height: 5-5; weight: Well, hell, I can lie a little there; hair: brown; eyes: brown... or maybe I should say 'dark amber'. Men like amber eyes, don't they? Or does that make me sound like a mountain lion?

Afterwards, Wendy made her stand up and snapped a couple of pictures. Suzanne wore three different outfits before she was satisfied with the digital image. Her new dark blue dress was the most flattering so she allowed Wendy to upload that picture, plus a simple face shot, to the email containing the completed questionnaire. Looking at her photo, Suzanne actually thought a man might consider her pretty.

"Okay, that's it. You ready?" Wendy's hand was poised over the "Send" button. Suzanne grimaced and nodded. Zing! The email vanished.

"Now your turn," Suzanne said, pouring her third glass of wine.

Fifteen minutes later, amid much giggling, Wendy's information, plus two photos that showed what a knockout she was, was sent to the mysterious stranger.

Suzanne had a sudden thought. "How long do you think it might take for them to get back to us?"

"Oh, I don't know. Maybe a week or so."

"Shit."

"What?"

"Well, if it is going to take that long, I should've subtracted another five pounds!"

Chapter Six

Brian looked with dismay at the pile of letters on his desk. "Rebecca!"

His secretary came in, a bemused expression on her face. "Yes, Brian?"

"What the hell is this? How am I supposed to get any work done?"

She came over and began flipping through the pile. "Well, as Confucius would say…"

"I know, I know, 'A journey of a thousand miles…' I just didn't expect such a response. There must be five hundred letters here!"

"Oh, that reminds me, you need to download your email." With that, she spun Brian's computer around and tapped a few keys. Brian sat there, eyes wide, mouth ajar, a look of dread on his face as his email box filled with line after line of responses.

"No! No! This is a nightmare!"

"Oh, stop," Rebecca responded. "You should be flattered. Look at all these women who want to meet you!"

Brian shook his head. "I'm sorry I ever started this. Let's just trash everything and move on."

Rebecca put her arms on his desk and leaned over. "Oh, no! I've gone to a lot of trouble to set this up. The least you can do is look through some of them. Come on, we both know what you're looking for."

Brian's eyes took on a crafty glint. "That's a good idea." He sat up. "That's a great idea!"

Rebecca stepped back, suspicious. "What do you mean?"

He smiled. "I'll look at some… *After* you sort through them for me."

His secretary stepped back again and brought her hands up. "That's not in my job description, Mr. Armstrong." The sudden use of his surname was not lost on Brian.

"It is now. You got me into this mess, you can help get me out. Besides, you know what I want better than I do, right? You've seen the mistakes I've made. This is your chance to play Cupid." He indicated the mail. "When you get all these sorted down to a reasonable number, call me."

Rebecca just shook her head and sighed. "You'd better get used to answering your own phones for awhile."

*****

Ten days later, Rebecca showed up at his office, beaming.

"What's this?" he asked, then paused. "You can't be done already."

"Oh, yes I can!" With a flourish, she deposited several letters on his desk. "Here are your finalists."

Brian flipped through the stack, looking at the photos first. Some were reasonably good-looking but none had the looks of a supermodel. For a moment, he was disappointed then he caught himself. He glanced at Rebecca.

She nodded, as if reading his mind. "I figured you'd go by looks alone. You men! That's what's been getting you into trouble all these years. You see a gorgeous woman, but you know almost immediately that her personality doesn't match yours. Mostly because she's strong-willed, like you. You date for a while anyway, hoping she'll change or that you were mistaken. Then, when it's clear she's not your type, you move on—to the next gorgeous woman and start all over again." She put her hands on her hips. "Don't you see? You need a real woman—one who is compatible to your, um, interests."

"My interests?" He smiled.

"You know what I mean. A submissive. You're a very strong-willed man, Brian, and some women are really attracted to that." She indicated the pile of letters. "In here, you'll find some of those women."

He looked through the stack again, this time reading the answers to the questions as he held the pictures in the other hand. He'd read, then stare at the photo, then read some more. Finally, he raised his eyes to his secretary.

"You may just have something here," he allowed.

* * * * *

Two weeks went by. Except for some idle speculation the first few days, Suzanne had quite forgotten about the ad. Wendy mentioned it once, to see if her friend had heard anything. Suzanne told her no and suspected Wendy was wondering why *she* hadn't heard—after all she *was* a knockout.

Both soon dismissed the experience as just a silly lark, like mooning someone from a car window. A little bit dangerous, but not likely to cause any real harm.

The middle of the third week, Suzanne got a surprising message in her email box from a Rebecca

Detwiler titled "Kept Woman". Her heart pounding, she opened it.

Suzanne – you've passed first round. The next step is a video meeting. Would you like to proceed? If so, call me at 613-555-1904.

Rebecca Detwiler.

Suzanne thought it had to be a joke. How could she have been selected? Surely, this mystery man had far more beautiful women than she to choose from. A second later, she was on the phone.

"Wendy Thomason! Did you see it?"

"What?"

"The email from Rebecca. Didn't you get it?"

"You're kidding! She wrote back? What'd she say?"

"They said I passed the first round, then asked me if I wanted to meet him in a video hookup!"

"Oh my God! Hang on, let me check my email." Suzanne heard Wendy fumbling around with her computer. She returned in a few seconds. "No, I've got nothing." She sounded disappointed.

"Well, it'll probably get there tomorrow. No way they'd pick me and not you."

"Yeah. Maybe. Like I always say, you sell yourself short. Maybe he likes dark, mysterious, beautiful women." Suzanne thought Wendy was being kind. "But I think that's great for you! You are going to call her, aren't you?"

"Well, I don't know. You think I should?"

Wendy snorted. "Of course I think you should! Are you nuts? Do you know how many women would kill to be in your shoes?"

Suzanne had trouble believing her good fortune. "Yeah, I suppose. I just wish you'd get your email, too, so we could do this together."

"Together! Girl, he doesn't want a twin act, he wants a girlfriend. If you play your cards right, you might get laid."

Chapter Seven

Sam sat in his car outside the Blue Bayou Co. warehouse, smoking cigarettes. He'd been sitting there since nine-thirty, parked in a lot across the street, just waiting to see if his information would prove to be correct.

It hadn't been hard to find out the location of Suzanne's job. Armed with her Social Security number—after all, he had been married to her for four years—Sam paid a few bucks to an Internet web site. Within a day, he had the address of her new apartment, her workplace, information about a used car she'd purchased since their divorce and even details of a parking ticket she'd failed to pay.

Now he had to be careful. He had no desire to go back to jail. Yet, just leaving her alone didn't occur to him. She had put him in that jail, ruined his life. She would have to pay. The question was, how?

"These things must be handled *del-icately,*" he cackled, like the Wicked Witch on *The Wizard of Oz*. "*Del-icately.*"

He spotted some activity across the street. People were streaming out for lunch. Sam checked his watch. It was ten minutes past noon. If she left, he should be able to spot her immediately.

Surreptitiously, he eased the small binoculars to his face and scanned the crowd. It didn't take long. Within three minutes, Suzanne strolled out.

"Gotcha, you bitch." His eyes followed her as she went to the parking lot and slipped into her car, a faded blue Dodge.

He was impressed—he hadn't remembered Suzanne looking so good before. "Whadcha do, get one of them TV makeovers?" he muttered to himself. He started up his car and drove to the attendant's shack, keeping an eye on the blue car. As he pulled alongside the window, he looked back to see Suzanne turn right into traffic, heading south on Third Street.

Sam paid his ticket and sped out after his ex. He caught up to her three blocks down and followed cautiously, slouching down in the seat in case she looked too closely in her rearview mirror. His car was different from the one he had when they were together so he hoped her eyes would just slide right off of it.

She parked outside a mall and entered. Sam parked a row over and down a few spaces, then followed her inside. He'd have to be careful—if she spotted him, it'd be all over.

Quite a few shoppers filled the mall. Sam hung back, letting his eyes rove around until he saw Suzanne entering a shoe store. He waited, staying out of sight, wishing this sissy state didn't ban smoking in every goddamn building.

Suzanne came out suddenly and turned left, away from Sam. He watched for a moment then slipped into the foot traffic behind her. His brain recorded everything automatically, helping him to answer the questions that he needed to decide what to do with his ex-wife. *Where does she go? Who does she see? Does she have a boyfriend? Does she live alone?*

*****

The voice on the line was prim, professional. "Rebecca Detwiler." That was it—no company name or other information that might give away the mystery man's true identity.

"Hel-hello," Suzanne said, glancing over at Wendy. She'd made Wendy come over before she'd agreed to call. She could never have done it on her own. "This is Suzanne, I'm one of the finalists. I, uh, have some questions."

"Yes, Suzanne Montgomery? I'm so glad you called."

"You are?"

"Oh, yes. My boss was very taken with your questionnaire."

Suzanne recoiled. *Is she just saying that?* "That's what I wanted to talk to you about. You see, I'm really very nervous about all this. I'm very concerned that this is all just a scam. That you'll either ask me for money or you'll—your boss—will start stalking me."

"Yes, that's the same thing I hear from some of the other finalists. Several of them dropped out because of it, sorry to say."

"Really?"

"Yes, of the thirty finalists, so far just twenty-two have responded. Eight of them said they felt they made a mistake and asked that they be taken off the list and left alone. I wish I could have convinced them that this is all on the up-and-up."

"But how can you? I mean, you're just a voice on the phone. You could be anyone. Maybe Mr. Big doesn't exist. Maybe this is some teenager's sick joke. You know, a lot of women could be hurt."

"Oh, we're aware of it. I told Mr., uh, my boss that this probably wouldn't work. But he's just been so depressed lately, meeting women who, um, weren't his type. He thought he might, just might, meet what he calls 'a real woman' this way."

"Then why advertise for a 'kept woman'? That begs for gold-diggers."

"Yes, but that's what he wants. He's definitely an Alpha Male, but in a good way, I'd say. He wants a woman who enjoys being kept—as long as it's for the right reasons."

"And what reasons are those?"

"Oh, I'd better let him tell you all that. Would you like to meet him via a video conference?"

"Uh..." She looked over at Wendy, who nodded emphatically. "Yes, I guess I would."

"You don't sound positive."

Wendy was giving her the evil eye, as if to say, "Don't you blow this!"

"No, I want to. I'm just a little scared, that's all."

"That's understandable, but completely unnecessary. He's a perfect gentleman, I can assure you."

"How many other women will be meeting him?"

"We've narrowed it down to twenty-two. If we need to, we have many more."

"Really? You had a good response?"

"Oh, yes. I'd say fifteen hundred women wrote in."

Suzanne was suddenly very impressed that she had made it. "And all those women really filled out those embarrassing questionnaires?"

"Yes, they did. I suppose they were curious, just like you."

"This sounds like a hell of a lot of trouble to go through for a date."

"I agree. But it does cut through a lot of wasted time as well. Don't you think so?"

Suzanne was reassured by the woman's candor. "Yes, I guess so."

"So you'd like to meet with him?"

Suzanne could feel Wendy's eyes on her. "Yes. Yes, I would."

They arranged a time and place convenient to both schedules and Suzanne agreed to show up at the Kinko's with all her questions and concerns.

She started to hang up, but then another question occurred to her. "Oh, I wanted to ask—my friend Wendy also applied and didn't make it out of the first round."

Now it was Wendy's turn to blanch. Suzanne leaned in so her friend could hear Rebecca's side of the conversation.

"She's a beautiful girl—I was wondering if you can tell me why she was rejected," Suzanne said, smiling at Wendy's discomfort.

"I can't discuss why certain people didn't make the cut. I can only say that my boss has certain criteria and for whatever reason, your friend didn't meet them."

"But she's a wonderful woman!" Beside her, Wendy nodded vigorously in agreement.

"I'm sure she is. But my boss is looking for a particular type. For whatever reason, she didn't answer the questions in the way he wanted. As I've said, we had more than fifteen hundred responses. We had to trim it down somehow."

Suzanne thanked the woman and hung up.

"You didn't have to do that!"

"Oh, you don't like it when the shoe's on the other foot, huh?"

"I didn't care that he rejected me—I was only doing it to get you to do it."

"Sure you did. You can't fool me—I know you were disappointed not to be picked."

"Yeah, I was." Wendy sat back and had another sip of wine. "What am I, chopped liver? I thought my answers were very inventive!"

"There's no accounting for taste," Suzanne said, secretly pleased that for the first time in their lives, she had been considered more desirable than Wendy. Not that she could really believe it.

"Well, I'm glad you took the initiative at least."

"Maybe it's the 'new me' coming out, hmmm?"

"I'll bet the Sugar Daddy would like the new you as well. When's your big TV production?"

"What? Oh, that. Tomorrow at nine. I'll have to call Glenda at work, tell her I have a dentist appointment or something."

"Do you know what you're going to say?"

"Uh, no. I'll just be myself." Suzanne suddenly began to feel uncomfortable with the topic, as if by merely mentioning it, she'd jinx it. She changed the subject. "How about you, have you answered any personal ads lately?"

"Oh, maybe." She gave an enigmatic smile.

"Wen! Come on, fess up!"

"Okay, I did answer an ad a few days ago…"

"Show me! I've got the paper right here!"

Reluctantly, Wendy thumbed through the tabloid and ran her fingers down the columns of personals. "Here it is—I see you circled it too! Did you respond?"

Suzanne hung her head. "Um, no. But he did sound nice, didn't he?" She read the ad to herself again:

SWM, 40ish, tall, seeks adventurous, funny, sexy woman for good times, travel and candlelight dinners…

"Did you hear anything?" Suzanne asked.

"No, not yet. But he's probably gotten hundreds of responses."

"You should send in a photo—that'll put you at the head of the line."

"I don't want to lure him with simple physical beauty," she huffed dramatically. "I want him to love the inner woman!"

"Wen, you crack me up."

Chapter Eight

The next morning, Sam sat in his car, a half-block down from Suzanne's apartment building, nervously jingling his keys. It was a quarter to nine, so she should be leaving any moment now.

There! He spotted her crappy blue car heading out of the driveway. She turned right, away from him and sped off up the street. Sam waited, smoking cigarettes and jingling his keys for another fifteen minutes, in case she came back for some forgotten item.

Finally satisfied, he stepped out of his car. He wore a black Giants ball cap and faded green coveralls with the words, "Jake's Repairs" on the back. They reminded him of his hated jailhouse jumpsuit, but he needed the disguise. He wanted to be invisible.

Carrying a toolbox, he bypassed the front door. Like many apartments in San Francisco, visitors had to be buzzed in at the front door. But Sam had checked out this building carefully. He knew the service entrance was often left unlocked and at 9 a.m., the super was probably still stumbling around his apartment, trying to wake up.

Sam reached the back door and turned the handle. It was locked. *Dammit!* Then, as an afterthought, he pulled hard on the door. It squeaked, caught in the jamb for a moment and came open. Slick.

He eased through, and looked around. The corridor was empty. He found the stairs to the second floor, where he knew Suzanne's apartment was located and climbed as quietly as he could. If he passed someone, he planned to walk by as if he owned the place and hoped his appearance would go unnoticed.

His luck held. He reached Suzanne's apartment without spotting anyone. Most residents had already gone to work. He squatted down and opened the toolbox. He removed the new Keymaster battery-operated lock pick and threaded the narrow prongs into the keyhole. The damn thing made too much noise, but in less than ten seconds, he heard the pins fall into place and he opened the door. Grabbing his toolbox, he slipped inside.

He looked around her neat apartment and had a strong desire to ransack it. Break things. Pee on the carpet. Rip up her clothes. But he wasn't there for that. Opening the toolbox again, he removed a small listening device, the size of a credit card, only a little thicker. He looked around, trying to decide the best spot. The coffee table was not far from the phone on an end table so that would be perfect, he decided. He flipped a tiny switch on the side of the card and a small green light glowed. That would never do. Taking a piece of electrician's tape out of the toolbox, he fastened a small piece over the light.

Peeling the backing off of sticky tape on one side of the bug, he knelt down and attached it to the underside of the table. She wouldn't see it unless she happened to lie on the floor, so it should be safe for a few days.

A few days were all he needed.

He took a radio receiver out of the toolbox. He plugged in the single earpiece, attached it to his ear, before holding the radio up and away from him. Stretching out, he reached the table and tapped his fingernails on it. In his ear, he heard the clicking sound. Nodding, he got up, put the radio away and quietly left the apartment, making sure to lock it on the way out.

* * * * *

A few miles away, Suzanne nervously stood outside the Kinko's, trying to gather her courage to walk inside. It was ten minutes before her scheduled interview with Mr. Big and she was petrified. Rebecca's email had admonished her not to bring any friends with her so Wendy stayed home. She could use her right about now, Suzanne thought. Wendy would give her a push.

Taking a deep breath, she pulled open the door and went inside. She strode with more confidence than she felt to the desk.

"May I help you?" The clerk was a tall black woman with hair pulled so tightly into a frizzy ponytail Suzanne wondered if it served as a cheap facelift.

"Yes. Yes. I'm Suzanne Montgomery and I have an appointment to use the video-conferencing room."

"Oh, yes, Miss Montgomery. This way, please." She led her back to a small room that had a rectangular table and two folding chairs. Two more chairs were stacked against the wall. Opposite the table sat a large TV screen with a camera on top. Suzanne's stomach fluttered.

"I think there's someone there now," the woman said and clicked on the set. In a few seconds, Suzanne saw an image of another, more formal room. A middle-aged blonde woman sat behind an ornate desk. She was dressed in expensive clothes and seemed poised and intelligent.

"Hello," the black woman called. "Can you hear us okay?"

The image nodded. "Yes, just fine." She looked in Suzanne's direction. "You must be Suzanne?"

"Um, yes."

The black woman indicated that Suzanne should sit down. "Just press this red button if you need anything and I'll come right in."

Suzanne sat as the clerk left. "Are you Rebecca?"

"Yes, I am. I'm so glad to finally meet you. I know this all seems so strange."

"Yes, I'm rather nervous."

"We'll talk for a minute to get you relaxed. You'll have a few minutes to chat and perhaps assure yourself that he's legitimate. Ask any questions you want to. Anyone who passes this level will get to meet him in person, on a real date. My boss said he's looking for between five and ten finalists out of the twenty-two women."

"How will he determine who to cut?"

"The same way you can talk to someone at a party and determine whether or not you're compatible in the first few minutes. Some people click and others don't. I think you'll know one way or the other at the end of the interview." She looked off screen for a moment and nodded.

"Okay, my boss is here now so we're ready to go. Are you ready?"

Suzanne suddenly lost her voice so she just nodded. She wished she had thought to bring in a glass of water.

"Hello, Suzanne." He appeared suddenly onscreen. Suzanne couldn't help but stare, speechless.

The man was a hunk. He was tall and full through the chest, as if he still worked out regularly. He had dark hair with speckles of gray at the temples, wide blue eyes with tiny crinkly lines around the edges—he could have been a runway model. She could picture him in an Armani suit, striding confidently through a crowd of celebrities at Cannes, or toasting a candidate for the Senate at a Washington D.C. fundraiser.

In some ways, he looked like an older version of Superman. He had the same square jaw, the same kind eyes, the same sardonic smile, as if he had a secret. He stood about six feet tall, she guessed. He wore a blue polo shirt, open at the collar. There was some logo on the shirt, but she couldn't read it onscreen.

The image smiled at her. "You must be Suzanne. Let me introduce myself. I'm Brian Armstrong, president of Armstrong Control Systems."

Suzanne had never heard of him or his company. She struggled to find her voice. "Um, I'm, uh, pleased to meet you."

"Thanks. Are you all right?"

"Oh, sure. It's just a little strange is all."

"I can appreciate that. It's strange to me too."

"Why do it?" she suddenly blurted. "If you're as rich as Rebecca says, you should be able to have any woman you want."

He looked directly into the camera. Suzanne felt he was gazing into her soul. "It's not easy meeting women in my circles." He stopped. "That's not right. I mean, I meet women everywhere but they too often carry with them certain expectations."

"Such as?"

"Mainly a sense of entitlement. They want the best restaurants, the most exotic travel spots, the most expensive jewelry. After all, that's what they've been used to all their lives."

"But surely you could find a waitress or a flight attendant or someone who isn't rich who'd love to go out with you."

"Yes, I can. And many of them are so thrilled to be going out with a rich man that I feel like they're really going out with my wallet. I could just stay home."

The mental image caused Suzanne to laugh.

He seemed relieved at her reaction. "You have a very nice laugh, Suzanne."

She blushed. "Thanks. Uh…getting back to that point, though, with all these ads and questionnaires from a mysterious millionaire, aren't you just asking for women who want to date your wallet?"

"Perhaps. I'm hoping I'll be able to find that one special gem among the rhinestones."

Suzanne shook her head. "What made you think I might be that person?"

"Let's say I was intrigued by your answers to the questionnaire."

"Really?" Suzanne could feel herself blushing. "It took three glasses of wine to get through it."

"Well, I'm glad you did."

"So what was it that made you put my file in with the beautiful blondes and models?"

"Oh, is that how you think I made my selections? I shouldn't be surprised—after all, you don't know me. But it's a fair question. I loved your responses. There was an honesty there that I've rarely found."

"Speaking of honesty, I must tell you, I had some serious misgivings about answering. My friend Wendy convinced me to take a chance. I'm not normally like that."

"Really? Why not?"

"Oh, I guess I'm just more shy, more reserved. She's more of a free spirit."

"I can appreciate that. I guess I like the shy, reserved types." He smiled, showing even white teeth.

Suzanne wondered what it might be like to kiss that lovely mouth. She bit her lip, trying to focus. "Now, Brian. About that questionnaire. It was really over the line, don't you think?"

"How so? I was trying to gather information as quickly as possible."

"Yes, but so far, you have given us nothing of yourself, other than the barebones stats of your life."

"Yes, that's true. I'm being cautious, just like you. So what would you like to know?"

Suzanne smiled and reached down into her purse. "Well, I just so happen to have a questionnaire here…"

Brian laughed out loud. "See? I knew you were a real personality. Go ahead, fire away."

She started at the top, reading the embarrassing questions one after another. To his credit, Brian didn't flinch. He answered them without apparent evasion. A more complete picture of this intriguing man began to emerge.

He was born into a wealthy family, so he'd always enjoyed rank and privilege, yet he had a burning desire to make it on his own. He avoided his father's business to start his own and has made it a success through hard work and occasional good luck.

On the personal side, Brian told her he'd lost his virginity when he was fifteen to the blonde princess next door who was a year older. Her parents found out and there was quite the hue and cry over it. While he had been smitten, the girl soon moved on to more mature conquests, breaking his heart, temporarily.

He liked to be dominant in his sexual relationships, a trait that seemed to fit his forceful and forthright personality. He even enjoyed a little bondage and discipline in his sex games, although not to a great extent. The thought made her tingle inside for reasons she couldn't fully explain.

"I wondered about this 'kept woman' ad that you ran in the city. It seems contradictory. From what you've said, you don't want a woman like that, who will lie around the pool or go shopping, except for when she's needed to…er…make love to you. Do you want to keep your woman like a pet?"

He paused, then said, "No, but I don't want her to try to control my life either."

"How do you mean?"

"You'll probably think I'm a caveman, but I'm tired of the constant battle for supremacy that goes on in most relationships today. I can't blame women for wanting more control—I just don't want to give up mine. When you have two people who are equal in a relationship, you end up constantly fighting turf wars. I want a woman who won't mind being 'kept', and by that I *don't* mean demeaned or abused. She should be the kind of woman who enjoys letting the man be a man. Does that make sense?"

"Yes, in a way. But this sounds like just the kind of gold-digger that you say you don't want. You know—some woman who is willing to be bought off. If you ever ran out of cash, she'd be gone."

"It's a fine line, I admit," Brian paused, and then blushed. "I'm looking for a woman who expresses certain attributes. I want a, um, demure woman."

Suzanne understood his point. She loved strong men, but most of the strong men she knew were arrogant jerks or control freaks like Sam turned out to be. Could Brian be different?

"What do you think about that?" he pressed.

"I guess I'm a little worried that you'll be very controlling. That I'd lose my sense of self."

"No, that's not what I want at all. I'm going to a lot of trouble to find the right kind of women for me—I don't want her to be a simple, um, love-machine. I want a full-functioning, honest, earthy woman who really cares for me and not just my money."

"And you haven't found that so far? I imagine you've been dating quite a while." Idly, she wondered how this man could've avoided a serious relationship before now. Was he too picky?

"Yes, I've been dating for about twenty-five years. And no, I haven't found 'Ms. Right'. Now I find myself tired of the 'hit-or-miss' efforts of hoping the next lady I meet in a bar or social event will be well-suited for me."

"I know what you mean. I don't seem to have had much luck, either. In fact, when I met my so-called 'Mr. Right', he turned out to be Mr. Wrong."

Brian asked her about her relationship with her ex-husband and she gave him the barebones explanation. She didn't tell him Sam was in jail for assaulting her, only that he had become abusive and she had divorced him. *Why go into the grisly details?* she thought.

"That's what scares me now—that I could've been so wrong about somebody. How can I trust my own judgment?" She bit her lip, afraid she'd said too much. But she was just being honest.

Brian absorbed that for a few seconds. When he spoke again, his voice was subdued. "No, you're right to be cautious. Hell, this probably won't work," he said, waving his hand in the air. "What the hell. I'll probably end up marrying some daughter of a polo pony-owning patron of the arts who feels it's her birthright to get suntans and spend her husband's money." She could hear him sigh.

Marriage? Who said anything about marriage? Suzanne thought.

As if they both felt they had skirted too close to some sensitive subjects, they steered away toward more innocuous chatting. She found out he owned a cat named Charlie, which had surprised her because he seemed like a dog person.

"Nah. I like dogs too, but I travel a lot so I can't keep one. Cats can fend for themselves for a few days if you leave them plenty of food and water."

They stayed on safer ground until the time was nearly up. "Well, we're about out of time. Do you have any other questions before we go?"

"Um, well, let's see…" Suzanne's mind locked up. She had one question she'd failed to ask so far and it burned in her. But how could she ask it?

Brian seemed to sense her hesitation. "Why don't you ask the one question that's forefront on your mind?"

His directness caught her unaware. She blurted it out before she could stop herself. "Okay, why me? What made you pick a slightly overweight brunette out of a crowd of thin, beautiful blondes?" Suzanne felt the prickly heat of embarrassment flow from her chest up to her cheeks. She was sure he could see the red flush, even through the TV. She held her breath, waiting for the answer.

"Good question. Of course, you're assuming that I only like thin blondes. I'm not quite that shallow." He laughed and shook his head ruefully. "I liked the answers you gave and you're a very pretty woman. You looked very real to me, if that makes any sense. There was something about your smile. Enigmatic, perhaps. Like Mona Lisa. I had to learn more about you."

Wow. She felt her blush deepen. He was starting to make her wet. She squirmed uncomfortably. She felt faint. No one had said something like that to her that before, not even Sam.

"By the way," Brian said. "You look terrific in that dress."

She blushed anew. "Thank you. I just got this the other day."

"For this?"

"Actually, no," she lied. "I got it to go with my new haircut and, um, diet."

"Well, you look very nice. I really enjoyed talking to you."

"Goodbye, Brian. Good luck on finding the perfect woman. I mean…"

"I know what you meant." He seemed ready to say something else then stopped himself. "Rebecca will be in touch. Goodbye, Suzanne, I really enjoyed meeting you." The screen went dark.

Shakily, she got up from the table and managed to get out to her car without fainting or throwing up. She was on her cell phone before she put the key in the ignition.

"Wen? Hi. Just got done."

"Well, how'd it go? Is he nice?"

"Veeerrry nice. Too nice." She described him and some highlights of their conversation.

"Holy shit!" Wendy exclaimed when she was finished. "He sounds like a dreamboat. Rich, handsome and he likes you."

"How can you say that?! It's way too soon." But secretly, she hoped Wendy was right.

"Oh, come on, you can tell, can't you? All women can tell when a man's interested in them. I say you scored big points!"

"You really think so?"

"Just you wait."

Chapter Nine

Rebecca couldn't help but notice the smile on Brian's face when he came out of the conference room.

"That must've gone well. I don't see you smiling that often after your video interviews."

"Yeah, I like her. She's...um, quiet and smart and real."

"Good. I was hoping you'd put her on the short list."

"Really? Why? You didn't listen in, did you?"

"Oh, no, I wouldn't—that's private. I'm just saying from my talks with her, she's intrigued. And she seemed a good fit for you."

"So you think she's..."

"Submissive? It's all right, you can say the word out loud. Yes, I'd say she is, definitely. Look at her answers! She'd be a good fit, I think."

"Really?" Brian mulled that over. "Good. She intrigues me as well. There's just something about her I can't explain...some X factor."

"I think it's a mutual attraction. You guys are both checking each other out. You really need to go on a date with this woman, just to see."

"Yeah." His eyes drifted off for a minute. Then he shook himself. "Okay. Who's next?"

Later that evening, Brian sat on his couch, a chilled martini in one hand and mulled over his meetings that day. Of the eight women, six were forgettable—not that they weren't lovely people in most cases, but simply because he felt no chemistry with them. One woman in particular, Diane, had seemed overeager and had reminded Brian of the obsequious hangers-on who would sacrifice their souls to live the life of luxury. He shuddered involuntarily. Sorry, Diane.

The two that interested him, Barbara and Suzanne, were as different as night and day. Barbara was the sunny blonde, carefree and savvy. Suzanne was the dark horse candidate, shy and cautious, yet with a smoldering sexuality that couldn't be hidden. Of the two, Brian felt the strongest visceral attraction to Suzanne. There was something about her that appealed to him. It wasn't just her sexiness, it was her honesty. She clearly had been nervous, yet curious. After they had talked for a few minutes, Brian felt the connection that he'd been searching for.

Even now, as he thought about her, he could feel his cock stirring. He smiled down at his lap. "Whoa, fella, don't get too excited. We've got lots of women to see yet."

He shook his head. Here he was, a grown man, talking to his penis. He took another sip of his drink and tried to put all of the women out of his mind. Just for now. Just to help clear his head. He stood and went to the kitchen to freshen his drink. His cock caught in his pants and he tugged at his belt. His balls ached.

Brian returned to the couch, fresh drink in hand and absently allowed the image of Suzanne to return to his thoughts. Yes, she was special. To look at her, you wouldn't think so, he told himself. She was pretty enough, sure. Maybe a tad overweight but that didn't bother him. It was the way she moved, even while sitting down—the movement of her shoulders, her head. Like she had a secret she wanted to share with him. *Or am I just crazy?*

Unconsciously, his hand reached down to stroke his cloth-covered cock. Jeez, he was hard. He couldn't remember the last time a woman did this to him. For a moment, he tried to concentrate on Barbara, the blonde. She would be worth dating as well, but his softening cock told him she didn't have the power to arouse him like Suzanne did. He wondered why some women affected him like that, while others didn't. Was it simply chemistry?

He sipped his drink, allowing himself to fantasize about Suzanne once again. Their date would probably start out quietly—a dinner, a few drinks. He wondered if she was submissive, as Rebecca had said he needed in a woman. He'd never really thought about it before, but he supposed he'd been thinking it without putting it in those terms.

Brian fantasized about Suzanne. Maybe she would be the type of woman who could enjoy letting him be the "master" of the house. He chuckled at the thought. He visualized coming home to a woman who could anticipate his needs. She'd be waiting there by the door, wearing a skimpy outfit, holding a chilled martini in one hand. She'd ask about his day and actually pay attention to what he had to say. She'd tell him she made dinner—or ordered it from a takeout. He wouldn't care, as long as she took good care of him. Hell, for that kind of attention, he'd gladly support her. And nurture her and love her as well.

Or am I just a male chauvinist pig?

His cock didn't care. It remained rock-hard, thinking about it. Still, he was a modern man. Would he get bored with a woman like that? Was he so shallow that he only wanted a shell of a woman? Would he value her less if she didn't stand up for herself?

He couldn't answer those questions right now. Maybe after he got to know her. But right now was the time for fantasy, he decided. Enjoy it because it's often fleeting.

His hand returned to his cock and he rubbed it absently, enjoying the sensations rolling through his loins. His balls needed release. He took a final swallow of his martini and put the glass down. Unzipping his pants, he allowed his engorged cock to spring free. For some reason, he felt like a horny teenager again. Shrugging, he decided "what the hell".

His fist began to stroke his hardened shaft, slowly at first, visualizing Suzanne kneeling between his legs, her lips partially open, eyes inviting. She would want to put her lips around his cock, but would wait to be asked. Or told. His thoughts were a jumble as he rubbed himself, faster and faster. His eyes rolled back in his head and he imagined it was Suzanne's mouth causing the friction he felt. Or her hot, wet pussy. She might squat over him, pressing his cock into her, riding him for all she's worth.

Brian could feel his balls twitching now, readying for release. His hand kept up its steady pressure. He closed his eyes, seeing Suzanne riding, or sucking or…

He cried out as a rope of cum peppered his shirt. He didn't care. His head lolled back against the cushions and he waited for his breath to return to normal. *Wow*, he thought. *That was pretty hot for a girl I haven't even dated yet!*

*****

Suzanne was surprised when the call came from Rebecca—no more email, she was getting personal calls.

She thought she'd ruined everything, though Wendy had thought otherwise.

"Suzanne? You're in. You're one of the seven finalists."

"Wow. I'm…well, I'm stunned."

"Why?"

"I thought I came on too forcefully when I talked to Bri—Mr. Armstrong. You know, he wants a more docile woman…"

"Oh, he's a lot more complex than that. If you ask me, he's just looking for a good fit. All this talk about a kept woman—I think it might've gotten in the way a little bit."

"How do you mean?"

"He doesn't want a woman who simpers and swoons in his presence or has no life without him. I believe he wants a woman who simply sees the world the way he does and enjoys letting him be a man."

Suzanne expected there was more she wasn't saying. The question was, did she want to find out? "So what happens next?"

"He'll call you himself within two weeks."

As soon as she hung up, she was on the phone to Wendy. Her girlfriend shrieked so loudly, Suzanne had to hold the phone away from her ear.

"That's mar-vel-ous," Wendy said, "just mar-vel-ous!"

"He's going to call me in two weeks. That doesn't give me much time to lose five more pounds!"

"Heck, don't bother—sounds like he likes you just the way you are."

"Yeah, right—I know I'm up against a bunch of skinny blondes. I need a little edge."

"Oh, pshaw. You look good, really good. I've been thinking of putting the moves on you myself."

"Oh, hush. I think I need another dress, though. You think?"

"Another dress couldn't hurt. Something really sexy. Make him want to rip it off of you."

"Stop, now—that's your style."

*****

Twelve days later, Brian called Suzanne. She had just come in from work and was exhausted, but hearing his voice cheered her up immediately.

"Suzanne? Brian Armstrong. I'm glad you agreed to take my call. Would you like to have dinner with me?"

"Oh, sure, Brian. I'd love to. It will be nice to finally meet you in the flesh." As soon as she said it, her blush returned. "I mean…"

Brian swept past her unintentional *double entendre*. "And I'm really looking forward to meeting you. How about Friday night, say seven? My limo will pick you up."

"Yes, that would be fine. Friday, then." She hung up.

Suzanne called Wendy. "He called," she said simply when her friend answered.

"Oh, my god, I'm so jealous. And horny! You're going to have to tell me everything. Maybe I could come along and be a chaperone or something."

"Ha ha. Wen, I'm terrified—do you think he'll like me, I mean really like me?" Suzanne couldn't help but get her hopes up, having come this far.

"Of course—who wouldn't love you? You look great and you're a great person. He must see that!"

Suzanne smiled. She had shed more than fifteen pounds in the last few weeks. Her work kept her from the gym, but she found she could get quite a workout on the warehouse floor. Plus, she stayed away from fatty foods. She did feel good, dammit. Now if she only felt confident about it.

"Wen, what am I going to say? How should I act? This guy's a world traveler. He's so sophisticated, he probably knows what each utensil is for at a formal dinner. I'm going to look like Ma Kettle."

"Who?"

"Never mind. I meant an old frump. The point is, I'm scared shitless. I need some 'class' lessons—fast."

"I don't think so. He's said all along, he doesn't want a phony gal. He's had enough of them. He wants a real American girl. That's you."

"God knows why. If I were him, I'd choose a nice French girl. Someone who could suck the skin off a lemon."

Wendy laughed. "Hell, men like women who play hard to get. If I were you, I wouldn't offer to blow him on the first date."

"Um, thanks. I'll keep it in mind."

Chapter Ten

"You looking forward to your date?" Rebecca asked as she stood in the doorway of her boss's office.

He smiled up at her from the desk. "Uh, which one?" he said casually. "Barbara? Sarah?"

"You know who I mean. Suzanne."

"Oh her." He feigned indifference. "Yeah, I am, but I'm trying not to get my expectations too high."

"Caution is good. But I have to say, she seems…well, right for you."

"What makes you think so?"

"Call it woman's intuition."

Brian didn't say anything for a moment. "Some of the others are very nice." But those were just words to say to be polite. Truth was, he did find Suzanne to be intriguing. Some of the others, well, they turned out to be gold-diggers or simply incompatible, despite his best efforts to be selective in the process.

"I like Barbara," he said defensively. He brought her face to mind—full lips, blue eyes, blonde hair. A beautiful woman, to be sure. Not quite as smart as Suzanne, but that would be to his advantage, wouldn't it? She wouldn't be as challenging that way.

Rebecca nodded. "She's nice."

"That seems a lukewarm endorsement."

Brian knew Rebecca was not afraid to speak freely. "I just think Suzanne has a little more on the ball," she said. "And if you ask me, she isn't after your money."

"But the money does affect their judgment, doesn't it?"

"It has to, of course. The trick is finding the one to whom it matters the least."

"What about Sarah? She's smart."

"Yes, and pretty too. But she seems a bit rigid. She doesn't seem as lusty as Suzanne."

Brian frowned. "You think so?"

"It will take a very special woman to be 'kept' by you."

He laughed. "You sound a little bit envious…or is that just my imagination?"

"Well." She shrugged and said no more on the subject. "There are women out there who enjoy being 'kept'. Being in the control of a handsome, caring and very rich man. You could say it's many a woman's dream."

"I didn't know John was rich."

"Oh, he's rich in ways you can't imagine," she said as she turned and left his office before Brian could ask her exactly what she meant, even though he had a good idea. He smiled and shook his head.

* * * * *

Sam met the man in an alley outside a bar in the seedy Tenderloin District. "You got it?" he growled.

The pale Irishman nodded. Sam had met him two nights ago at the bar. Someone had told him if you need a piece, look up Squeaky. When he'd asked how to recognize him, he had been told, "Just listen for his voice."

They'd been right. "Nine mil, just like you asked," Squeaky said in a high-pitched voice, like Michael Jackson sucking helium. His vocal chords had been ruined many years ago in a brutal disagreement over some merchandise. Up until then, he'd always been called Mikey. But there was no escaping his new moniker.

"Where did it come from?" Sam worried that it might have a "history". If the gun had been used in a murder, for example, he might be tied into it if he got caught with it later.

"Stolen, four years ago. Hasn't been used in any crime, if that's what you're asking."

Sam pulled some bills out of his pocket. "Six, right?"

"Yeah." He handed the gun over and counted the hundred dollar bills. "The clip's empty. I make it a habit of never sellin' guns with ammo. I'm sure you unnerstand why."

"Yeah." Sam shrugged. Ammo was no problem. He checked it out. A black-matte Glock with a rubber grip. Perfect. Holds eleven shots. He wanted to put every one into Suzanne's face.

But no. He'd have to be careful. The cops would immediately focus on the angry ex-husband. He'd have to set it up so he had the perfect alibi.

"You sure this works all right?" He thumbed out the clip and checked it for rust. It looked clean and recently oiled.

"Yeah, sure. I wouldn't be in business long if I sold someone a bad gun. I gotta lotta satisfied customers."

Yeah, Sam thought, *except for that guy who gave you that voice.*

"Okay." Sam tucked the gun into his waistband. Now he was officially violating his probation. Big time.

Squeaky nodded. "You ever need anything else, you can find me here." He threw a thumb over his shoulder at the bar and strode off down the alley.

Sam let his shirt hang over the gun and walked with a newfound swagger back to his car. He spoke out of the side of his mouth, gangster-style. "It's all coming together, Suzie baby, it's all coming together."

Chapter Eleven

The day of her date with Brian dawned bright with promise. Suzanne went to work, as usual, but told everyone in the office she wasn't about to stay past five tonight.

"Oh, hot date?" asked Glenda Sykes, the office manager, lifting an eyebrow. It turned her grin into a leer.

Suzanne smiled. "Maybe." She had to tell her something, or Glenda might find some last-minute job for her to do. Behind her back, the other employees in the office called her "The Good Witch" and not just because of her name. She could act nice, and then would stab you in the back at a moment's notice.

"Oh, tell me—is he handsome?"

"Yes, and richer than Midas." Suzanne knew Glenda wouldn't believe her.

"Oh, posh, Suze, you're just teasing me now."

"Okay, he's a guy I met at the supermarket. Runs the produce department. He seems nice, though."

Glenda grimaced and forced a weak smile. She patted Suzanne on the arm. "Don't worry, we'll get you out of here in time for your little date." She tottered off on her three-inch heels. Suzanne knew she wore them because the boss complimented her on her legs one day about two years ago. From that day on, Glenda wore high heels to accentuate her best feature, in the vain hope that Smyth might follow up and ask her to dinner. So far, it hadn't worked, but you had to give her credit—she had the patience of Job.

Work dragged by for Suzanne—her mind was elsewhere. It seemed twenty hours crawled by before she was finally on the road home. Wendy had volunteered to come over and help her get ready. Suzanne decided she'd be too nervous with Wendy there, but she appreciated the moral support.

She purposely did not eat much in the last week, just to see if she could shave a few more pounds off. She avoided the scale all week, just hoping the dial would jump rather than crawl to a lighter weight.

When she got home, she stripped off her clothes and looked at herself in the full-length mirror in the bathroom. Her breasts were medium-sized and perky. She cupped them experimentally, as if offering them to Brian. Her hands dropped to her waist and pinched—the flab around her hips had mostly melted away. She half-turned and peeked over her shoulder. Her ass had firmed up as well. She flexed, watching the muscles contract. *A very fine booty, if I do say so myself,* she thought.

Finally, Suzanne approached the scale with some trepidation. She stepped on it, her eyes closed. Summoning all her courage, she looked down.

She had lost four more pounds.

Letting out a shriek, she called Wendy right away and told her.

"You won't recognize me, Wen. I might just blow away in the wind!"

"That's great! Oh, Suze, I'm so happy for you. You're gonna knock Brian's socks off. But I'm hoping it'll be his pants." She cackled.

"Oh, you talk a different game now. Just last week you said I shouldn't blow him on the first date!"

"And you were listening to me?"

"Okay, I gotta go get ready. I'll call you later and let you know how it went."

"You'd better. Otherwise, I'm going to camp on your doorstep."

A thought flashed through Suzanne's mind. "Hey, Wendy—do you think we oughta set up a signal or a prearranged call? You know, in case something goes wrong?"

"What? You mean, like, he kidnaps you and takes you to his mansion? Hell, you can call me and I'll take your place. That'd be like if Robert Redford offered you a million dollars to sleep with him—remember that movie? Thousands of women were thinking, 'Where do I sign?'."

"You know what I mean. Come on, I'd feel better."

Wendy wanted to laugh at her friend's fears, but she knew Suzanne had some legitimate concerns. "Okay, how's this. Bring your cell phone. I'll call, say, at ten—"

"No—nine-thirty."

"Okay, nine-thirty. If you are having a wonderful time and everything's going great, say, 'I'll have those reports tomorrow, Glenda.' Okay? If he's creeping you out or you want to end the date quickly, say, 'Mom, calm down—I'm sure Dad's going to be all right.' Then you can make up an excuse about a sick father you have to go to."

"Wen, my dad's been dead for six years—don't you think that will sound phony?"

"Okay, use your brother or your cat. I don't care. You wanted the out, not me."

"All right. All right. That sounds good." She drew a deep breath. "Wish me luck."

"Luck."

It took more than ninety minutes to get ready. Finally, Suzanne sat, nervously checking her freshly painted toenails before she slipped her feet into her new Prada shoes. For the tenth time, she went to the mirror and poofed her hair with her fingers. It was perfect. She smoothed her dark blue Vera Wang dress. Beautiful. She looked at her watch. Still ten minutes to go. She bared her teeth and checked for lipstick smears. Nothing.

"Well, maybe I'll just go to the bathroom one more time," she said aloud, even though she'd peed twice in the last hour. *Nervous bladder*, she thought.

She was washing her hands when she heard the doorbell ring. She looked up at her reflection, a stricken expression on her face. She shook her head. "Relax," she told her image. "Relax. It's just a date."

Taking a deep breath, she strolled ever so casually to the door. Opening it, she saw an olive-skinned man with a thin mustache waiting on the step. He wore a suit and carried a livery cap in one hand. Behind him, on the street, stretched a shiny black limousine.

"Ms. Montgomery?"

She nodded.

"I'm Baba, your limo driver. Are you ready to go?"

She nodded like a puppet, idly wondering if his first name was "Ali". Locking the door behind her, she patted her purse to make sure she had her cell phone and keys, then followed the man to the car. He opened the back door and helped her inside.

The compartment was empty. Suzanne sat back and took in the surroundings—a wet bar, a small video screen, a telephone. "Where are we going?" she asked when Baba settled in behind the wheel.

"To dinner at Elaine's," he said.

She nodded as if she went to Elaine's all the time. Truth is, she could never afford the four-star restaurant in the city's tony Mission District. Even getting a reservation was near impossible. She hoped she would be dressed appropriately.

Suzanne rolled down the panel at the wet bar, exposing a row of stoppered glass carafes, each etched with the name of a liquor—Scotch, Gin, Vodka and Brandy. She didn't want a cocktail, so she had a little water from the tiny faucet to wet her suddenly dry throat.

For a moment, as the car glided silently through the night, Suzanne nearly panicked, remembering all those movies where the innocent girl gets in the limo, expecting a wonderful evening, only to end up being driven to the deserted warehouse for God knows what torment. She whipped her head around, checking for landmarks and was calmed to see they were on Market Street, downtown's main thoroughfare. She breathed deeply and silently scolded herself for worrying.

Chapter Twelve

When Baba pulled up to the restaurant, Suzanne immediately recognized Brian standing out front. She checked her watch. Seven-twenty. She took another deep breath and tried to slow her racing pulse.

Brian opened the door and took her hand as she got out. He smiled. "You look wonderful tonight, Suzanne."

She nodded, too nervous to speak right away. Brian wore a dark pinstripe suit, light blue shirt and a yellow tie with little sailboats on it. He seemed very comfortable in his clothes.

"Please forgive me for not arriving at your door with Baba. I had a late meeting at work. Are you hungry?" He walked side-by-side, his head turned attentively toward her.

She wanted to say, "I haven't eaten all day, I'm starved!" Instead, she simply gave a soft "yes".

"The food here is pretty good," he said as he pulled open the heavy restaurant door.

"Ah, Mr. Armstrong," the maître d' said, smiling. "This way, please."

They were led to a private room, just large enough for three tables. The other two tables were empty.

"I thought we might have some privacy," he said. "I hope that's all right."

"Y-yes, it's fine," Suzanne murmured. He held the chair for her and she smoothed her dress and sat. The silverware glittered on the white tablecloth before her. She hoped she'd remember how to use all the utensils.

"I want to apologize for all the secrecy. I don't blame you for being paranoid." Brian sat across from her. He had an easy smile. Suzanne wanted desperately to believe that he had no hidden agenda.

I'm just being too suspicious, she scolded herself. *Lighten up!*

The waiter appeared, a short, balding man wearing a tuxedo shirt and a small white apron under his ample belly. "May I get you some cocktails before dinner?"

"Yes," Brian said at once. "Suzanne?"

"Um. I'll have a glass of Chardonnay."

"And a martini for me, on the rocks."

The waiter nodded and stepped away.

"So, how do you like your job?" A safe, innocuous question to begin the evening. Suzanne appreciated it as she wondered if there would be more, well, grilling was probably too harsh a word. Up to now, they'd seem to have been in a rush to find out everything about each other—him through the probing, personal questionnaires and her during the hurried conversations over the video hookup. Maybe now they could relax.

"Oh, it's okay. I mean, it's not my dream job or anything. It pays the bills." *Shit,* she thought. *He's going to think I can't wait to quit and have someone like him support me.* "How about yours?"

He laughed. "Well, being the boss makes it a lot more fun."

"Tell me how you started Armstrong…um…Control Systems. I'm curious."

He raised an eyebrow, as if asking, *Do you really want to know?* She nodded and he started… "After college, I was knocking about, trying to 'find myself'—"

The waiter appeared, interrupting him. He put down the drinks carefully and beat a hasty retreat. Brian took a grateful sip of his martini and smacked his lips.

"Anyway, no one seemed to want a mechanical engineer for some reason. Economy was pretty bad back then. I bounced around awhile and ended up working for a manufacturer of assembly line robots. It would've been a pretty good job if I'd been hired to design the robots, instead, I ended up on the line, fastening the bloody things together."

She enjoyed listening to him. Liked the way his eyes took on a dreamy quality while he reminisced. He absently rubbed the condensation off his glass with the flat of his thumb.

"While working there, I noticed how much trouble the company was having with their control equipment—you know, the computers that run the line or perform certain tasks, such as welding. The bossman said vendors were just throwing out crap into the marketplace to see what sticks. The software was giving us fits.

"I thought there would be a market for control equipment that ran on software designed from the ground up but that's expensive to do. No wonder vendors were selling first and designing second. With the arrogance of youth, I thought I could do better at developing a stable software platform, even though I wasn't a programmer. If I'd been any other Joe out there on that assembly line, that's as far as my thinking would've gone. But I had a secret weapon—my dad."

Suzanne remembered him telling her he had been born into a wealthy family. "Was he in electronics too?"

"No, real estate. But he had done very well for himself. I told him my idea and he was intrigued. I wanted him to bankroll me—but only under one condition—that he leave me alone for a full year before pressuring me to produce a product. He agreed."

"That must've been a whirlwind year for you."

"Yes, it was. I hired four guys from my college—all very sharp guys in computer science and engineering, all still out of work and hungry. We paid ourselves minimum wage, plus stock options. We sat around for six months talking over the problems before we wrote a single line of software. Then we came up with the best hardware configuration, mostly stuff we bought from vendors and modified, and started writing code for it."

"Did you meet the deadline you promised your dad?"

Brian smiled, a rueful grin that crinkled the right side of his face. "Hell, no. We blew past it by nearly another full year. We gave dad more stock options in an effort to keep him at bay. He told me I was going to bankrupt him and force him and my mother to live in a tent. Of course, he was exaggerating. Just about when he was ready to pull the plug on us, we invited him in to show him our demo model. He brought along a friend of his, a salesman for the biggest control systems manufacturer in the Mid-Atlantic."

Brian paused for dramatic effect. "They were impressed."

"Oh, come on! You've got to give me more details than that!"

His eyes met hers and for a moment, Suzanne felt a closer connection to him.

"Okay, the salesman was more than impressed. He told us he'd never seen anything that was so easy to use and was so adaptable. He said it blew away his own company's software. He was so excited, he quit and became our first salesman."

Brian shrugged. "The rest, as they say, is history."

"I'll bet your dad was happy."

"Yes. It took a few more years, and some close calls. But after we went public, the smile returned to his face. He made back his money many times over. Now he tells everyone, 'Oh, I believed in my son from the start.' What a liar." He said it with great affection. Suzanne could picture them sitting around a breakfast table, swapping lies and poking fun at each other.

"Both your parents are still alive?"

"Yes, and doing well. Dad's seventy now and Mom's a few years younger, but they're enjoying their retirement."

Brian drained his martini and looked over at Suzanne's half-empty glass. "Want another?"

"Yes, please." She didn't want to get drunk, but the wine helped calm her.

He picked up a small bell that she hadn't noticed before and rang it. Immediately, the waiter appeared, as if he'd been hovering around outside the door. "Another round," Brian told him and the waiter disappeared.

"Oh, we should've gotten menus by now, shouldn't we?" Suzanne asked, looking around the table.

Brian put his hand on hers. The move startled her. "I took the liberty of ordering dinner for us. I hope that's all right. I knew what you liked from your first questionnaire."

"Oh, um, that's fine." She liked the gesture—it just surprised her, that's all, she told herself. But her attention was on Brian's hand, still gently touching the back of hers. She didn't want to move it, lest she discourage him. But she wasn't sure if she was ready to encourage him, either. "So what are we having?"

"Let's let it be a surprise, hmm?"

She found herself nodding. With another man, she might've felt dismissed, but somehow she got a little thrill out of having Brian be in control. Perhaps it was due to the way he phrased his desires during their videoconference. She understood his point of view, respected it even, but wasn't sure if any man could handle the power of being in charge. Too many became cruel or abusive, a real turnoff. It took a rare man to find the balance.

Suzanne decided to wait and see, just wait and see. After all, she could bail out at any time. That's what her ego said, at any rate. Her id had a baser response—she felt that same tingle in her loins and nipples. Her mind tried to dismiss it. *Fucking cavewoman!*

"I'm sorry, what?" Suzanne came out of her reverie to see Brian staring at her.

"Nothing, really, I was just asking about your day. You seemed to be lost in thought."

"Oh, yes, um, I was just daydreaming for a second."

"Can I ask about what?"

"Um, just this strange situation. You know, how it's like 'The Bachelor' without the cameras." She looked around suddenly. "Unless…"

He grinned and held up his hands, palms out. "No cameras, I assure you. I'm too private a person for that."

Suzanne moved back to safer ground, asking Brian more about his life, his work, even some of his previous dates with the "polo pony-owning" crowd. She had to press him to talk about the latter, but when she did, she drew some insights into his quest for a soul mate.

"One time, I was dating this girl who was the daughter of a hotshot trial attorney," he said. "She lived in this big old empty house with her dad—her parents were divorced. I see the way you're looking at me, but she was no kid. Kate was twenty-six, and would move between her parents' homes depending upon her mood and how well she got along with each parent. So yeah, she was a little spoiled.

"She was amusing in small doses, so we dated for a few months. But she kept pressing me. She wanted to go to the best restaurants. That old Mexican restaurant down the street that served great, authentic food wasn't good enough—she wanted the white tablecloth treatment, the finest wines. I think she needed to be seen at those places, as if being rich was a competitive sport.

"Once I bought her a cameo on a little silver necklace, just because it caught my eye and I liked it. She thanked me, but I could tell she thought it unworthy of her for some reason. Maybe it wasn't the current fashion. She wore it for me that night, but I never saw it on her again." Suzanne could tell from the expression that it still bothered him.

"The end came not long after, when she wanted to go on vacation to Nice because some of her friends were going. She expected me to just up and take her. It wasn't that I couldn't afford it—I could. I just didn't like the idea of being at her beck and call."

"So why did you stick around her for so long?"

Brian pursed his lips, before shaking his head. "I'm sure you don't want to hear."

"Oh, you mean..."

"Yeah. She had some...talents." He laughed. Suzanne laughed too at her own naïveté. The thought, unbidden, flashed through her mind—*I'll bet she could suck the rind off a lemon.*

The waiter returned, bearing plates. Suzanne felt like a kid at Christmas, dying to see what he had ordered for her.

"For the lady," the waiter said, placing a dish before her with a flourish, "Trout Almandine."

Suzanne gasped and put her hand up to her mouth. "The story about my dad! You remembered!"

Brian nodded. As the waiter served him his food, Suzanne recalled the question that Wendy had answered for her—

What's your favorite memory of your childhood?

Trout fishing with my father on the Snake River. We'd fry up the fresh-caught fish right outside our tent and eat it with our fingers. Fish never tasted so good.

"Yes, I hope I guessed correctly."

Tears came suddenly to her eyes.

"What's wrong?" Brian said, suddenly concerned.

"No, it's okay. I just miss my dad."

"Oh," he nodded. "How long has he been gone?"

"Six years now. Mom was a lot younger than he was. He was forty-six when I was born. He used to call me his midlife crisis. He had a great sense of humor."

"I'm sorry if the trout—"

"No! It's wonderful! I'm going to eat every bite of this with great relish. If I cry a little now and then, those are tears of joy, you understand?"

Brian's smile grew. "Yes, ma'am. But I think I'd better let you pick your own dessert!"

She laughed. It was easy to be with Brian. They seemed to be on the same wavelength. She felt protected. "What did you order?"

"Filet mignon. I tend to spoil myself when I eat out. It's very good, too. Here, try a bite."

There was something intimate about the gesture. She leaned in as he held the fork steady, then steered the morsel into her mouth. It was warm and moist, and tasty. She offered him a bite of hers and he accepted it gladly. Her pussy began to announce its desire for some hot, heavy sex. She squeezed her legs together until the feeling abated.

They ate in silence for a while. Suzanne's trout was delicious. While her father never cooked anything as fancy as Trout Almandine under the stars, every bite reminded her of the experience.

When they were finished, they sat back like satisfied bears the night before hibernation.

Suzanne beamed. "That was excellent. Thanks so much."

"You're welcome. I enjoyed sharing it with you."

Suzanne let her smile fade. She debated asking the next question, yet it weighed heavily on her mind. "Can I ask you a question that might be a little unfair? I'm not sure of the rules of this game, after all."

"Sure, shoot."

"How many other women have you had dinner with so far? I mean, on your 'short list' of candidates?"

Brian paused. She could tell he was deciding how much to tell her.

"Four," he finally said.

"So I'm number five."

"Yes." He waited for the follow-up.

"Am I allowed to ask how the search is going?"

"You can ask, but I'm not sure how I'll respond. I mean, I'm not going to put you in a ranking, if that's what you mean."

"No, no! I'm just curious. How pleased are you with your selections, overall?"

"Hmmm. Some are very interesting, some are, um, less so." He paused. "And some are very intriguing." His eyes crinkled around the edges.

Suzanne wasn't sure if that was a good thing or not. *But at least I stand out*, she thought.

"Dessert?" The waiter had returned.

"Oh, not for me, I'm stuffed," she said.

"Just coffee for me," Brian told him, raising an eyebrow in her direction. She waved him off. The waiter cleared the dishes.

"Thanks for a nice evening," she said, trying to fill the silence.

"It's not over yet."

Did he mean – ?

"What else did you have in mind?" She knew she sounded a bit defensive. Why, she didn't know—her body certainly was responding to this handsome man.

Brian caught her tone. "No, no, your virtue shall remain intact, m'lady. I just mean, it's barely nine-thirty"

The rest of his words died away when her cell phone began chirping in her purse. Suzanne instantly knew who it was. She excused herself and fished the phone out.

"Hello?" She listened intently for a few moments. "No, I'll have those reports tomorrow, Glenda." She shook her head at Brian as if exasperated. She hoped he couldn't hear Wendy's delightful cackle just before she hung up.

"Work stuff," she said. "That was my supervisor."

"Uh-huh." Brian's lopsided grin told her he didn't believe her but it didn't matter.

Suzanne decided it best to change the subject. "Yes, it is early. We can stay and talk or…" She wondered if he planned to take her somewhere else or just drop her at home, perhaps glad to be rid of her.

"Actually, there's something else we could do, if you're game."

"As long as it doesn't involve a lot of athleticism. I'm too full."

Brian grinned. "Oh, I think you could handle it."

They dawdled while Brian drank his coffee. She could smell the cinnamon aroma, the steam rising from his china cup. She liked the way his hands held it. She pictured those hands touching her skin, stroking her.

Brian seemed normal so far, she decided, looking at him as he sipped at the hot liquid. As normal as rich people can be. This meal, for example, probably cost him what she earned in a week.

She didn't want to come across as greedy, yet she was curious about his lifestyle. *What kind of house does he have?*

What hobbies? Does he take limos to work or does he have a personal vehicle, perhaps a sports car? Where does he go on vacations? Each question that came to mind she rejected as prying. *Be patient,* her inner voice told her, *be patient.*

When it was time to go, Suzanne didn't see a check or any indication that Brian paid for their meal. *It must've been arranged ahead of time,* she thought. *He probably takes all his dates here.* She felt a pang of jealousy and immediately chided herself for it.

In the limo, Suzanne heard Brian murmur some words to Baba that she couldn't make out. Baba nodded and turned forward. A moment later, the privacy screen went up. Suzanne tried not to get nervous.

"Where are we going?"

"To a sporting event," he said, crinkling one side of his face. "But don't worry, you'll be able to handle this one."

Suzanne pondered his meaning for the next few minutes while the dark car moved through the streets like a spaceship. She could tell they were heading north.

Brian picked up the brandy and offered her a drink. She declined. She would've liked to have had a nightcap, but didn't want to lose any of her faculties right now.

Brian poured himself a small brandy and leaned back. "What do you look for in a man?"

The question took her by surprise. "Um, well, probably what most women want. Someone who's kind, intelligent, funny, successful…" Internally, she was thinking, *Someone who's not abusive, who isn't married to his work, or selfish, or arrogant…*

"How often do you find all those qualities in one man?"

She grimaced. “Not often. The balance, apparently, is hard to achieve.” The car glided onto the Golden Gate Bridge. Suzanne felt strangely comfortable with Brian. She decided to turn the tables. “What do you look for in a woman? Or should I know that already, from your questionnaire?”

Brian’s easy grin returned. “Yeah, I did pry, didn’t I? So you know I’m curious about a woman’s sexuality, her confidence, her beliefs. Can you forgive me for trying to take some shortcuts?”

“Not as long as you tell me what you expect in your ‘ideal woman’ that you seem driven to find in this rather unorthodox way.”

“Hmm. That’s kind of a question for the second date, don’t you think?”

“Does that mean there will be a second date?”

“It depends, doesn’t it? I’m on trial here as well, aren’t I? If I’m not sufficiently amusing or compatible, my wealth won’t matter, will it? Unless…”

“Unless I’m a gold-digger, right?”

He nodded.

“Well, do you think I am?”

“First impression? I’d say no. You seem honest and genuine, so far. Let’s see how you do out on the course. I think we’re just about there.”

The course? The car turned off the highway onto the exit for Sausalito. She sat up, curious. She knew there were a lot of boats moored here, was he taking her to his yacht? The car made another turn and stopped. Suzanne craned her neck and looked out the window at the sign above a small building—Wee Golf World.

She turned back to Brian in amazement. "You're taking me miniature golfing?"

"That's right. It's a crucial test of our compatibility. If you beat me…" He let the answer hang.

Suzanne laughed, a real laugh, not forced or hollow. She felt more at ease with Brian with each passing minute. "You're on, buster."

"Okay, but we have to make it challenging. We have to give each other a handicap." His eyebrows rose. "What would you give me?"

"You want me to pick *your* handicap?"

"Yep."

"Okay." She shrugged. From dinner, she knew he was right-handed. "You putt left-handed."

"Fair enough. Now it's my turn." He paused.

Suzanne couldn't imagine what he might ask. That she should putt left-handed too?

"How about this? You play without your panties." He watched her reaction.

Suzanne recoiled in the leather seat. At first, she was indignant. Then she quickly realized this was all part of his testing of her. If she became offended, she'd probably be eliminated.

How did she feel about it? She was torn. On the one hand, he'd made a bold request that staked out his position—*Here's what I like. What do you think about it?* She had a right to be offended. On the other hand, she could play this right into the lap of luxury, if she felt like going along, regardless of her views on the matter. She knew that was the "gold-digger" option. But she sensed he wanted to see if she would take the third path—give him her true feelings about it. And what did she think? She smiled. It sounded like a naughty way to play miniature golf—and a great way to get to know Brian better.

"What are the stakes?"

Brian smiled then shrugged. "How big do you want to make them?"

Suzanne was just as quick. "Not too big." *Not yet*, she thought. Her pussy clamored to be included in the discussion. She tried to ignore her sudden arousal. It wasn't easy. Despite her efforts to be a proper lady on her first date, she doubted she would stop Brian if he made a move on her, right here in the limo. She could feel his strength as if it were a tone that echoed in her bones.

He nodded, his eyelashes seemed prominent as he briefly closed his eyes. "All right, how about this— If I win, we have a second date…" He paused. Suzanne waited expectantly. "…then you come to it without *any* underwear on."

Suzanne sat back against the dark leather. Brian's fetish had become clear. As fetishes go, it wasn't so bad. In fact, she enjoyed being the object of this man's sexual interest. *It's been too long.* Her loins felt hot.

"And if I win?"

"What would you want?"

Suzanne knew what she wanted. She wanted to feel his hard cock sliding into her, his arms enveloping her. But that would be too easy—that's what he wanted as well. "I…I don't know." She couldn't get the image out of her mind. His naked body over her, the smell of him, his fingers rubbing against her hot skin…

"You want me to pick your prize as well?"

"Y-yes," she got out, her voice suddenly hoarse.

"Okay. If you win, I'll take you to my private island."

"Your private island?"

"Yes, it's up near Napa. We could do some wine-tasting."

Suzanne thought he'd be tasting more than that. "You're on."

Brian nodded slowly and asked, "Do you want me to turn away?"

She was brought back to the present. He wanted her to remove her panties. "It's not necessary," she responded. Tilting her legs to the side, Suzanne lifted up her hips, reached underneath her dress and hooked her fingers into the small bikinis. Quickly, she yanked them down her legs and off. She doubted he saw anything. She twirled the briefs around one finger and let go, they ended up draped over the scotch bottle in the wet bar. Glancing over, Suzanne saw the crotch held a damp spot. She looked away, hoping he wouldn't notice, and yet, wanting him to know how turned on she was. Brian raised his eyebrows and gave her a Jack Nicholson leer, giving Suzanne a giggling fit.

They climbed out. The miniature golf course had just a few patrons, as it was getting late in the season. Soon the fog would recapture the peninsula every night, sending people indoors. She could feel the cool air against her naked flesh between her legs. She liked the naughty sensation it gave her.

Brian paid and they took their putters to the first tee. Suzanne wiggled her hips, relishing the feel of her naked pussy underneath her dark blue dress.

Why does this excite men so? she wondered. Then the animal in her spoke up—*Screw it; go with it.*

They started out slowly, like two gunslingers circling one another, seeing who really was faster. Suzanne thought she might have more experience at the game, since she couldn't imagine Brian playing miniature golf regularly. Then again, he picked the game, so he was probably an expert putter.

The first hole, Suzanne won with a lucky shot, causing her ball to end up right next to the cup. Brian's awkward left-handed shot rolled down on a shelf behind the hole. Coming back, it took him two putts to finish. Suzanne was ahead.

He grinned at her. "Okay, you won one. Now let's get serious."

They played on. Suzanne actually forgot she wasn't wearing panties as she concentrated on the game. Brian buckled down and managed to go up two strokes by the half. Suzanne was determined to win, to show him that she could hold her own against him. She gained a stroke on the sixteenth hole and went into the final two holes just one stroke down.

She tried hard to win one of the last two holes, but Brian's putting remained cautious and accurate. When the putts dropped on the eighteenth, Suzanne had lost by a stroke.

"Okay, you agree to the terms?" he confirmed.

Suzanne nodded. She felt both embarrassed and exhilarated. Now she could feel the wind, moving the hairs of her pussy. Could she have an entire date without panties or a bra? She had to admit, it did something to her. If he only knew how wet she was right now.

He took her home. It was not quite midnight. She wondered if he might ask to come in. She was ready to say yes, and not because she was willing to use sex to win his heart. She really liked the man.

Brian walked her to the door. She turned, looking up at his piercing blue eyes. "Good night, Brian. I had a lot of fun." She hoped she sounded sincere because she *did* have fun, dammit!

Without a word, he leaned down and gently kissed her on the lips, once, then again. She liked the feel of his soft lips on hers, the faint taste of brandy on his breath. He seemed to know just how to kiss—not too rough, but not too light, either. An all-encompassing kiss. Just enough to sweep her heart away, make her forget her surroundings for a moment.

He reached down and let his right hand slide up along the outside of her thigh, pulling her dress up with it. She reacted, afraid someone might see her, and grabbed his forearm. But he was too strong. His hand briefly cupped the round globe of her naked ass then fell away.

It was a possessive move, a powerful statement. Suzanne felt her labia expand, her wetness grow. She wanted to ask him in, but waited for him to make the decision.

"Well, um, good night," she breathed, her lips an inch from his.

"Good night, Suzanne. I had a wonderful time. Thanks for going out with me."

Suzanne felt a pang of disappointment. *Aren't you going to fuck me?* She wondered if he could read her thoughts in her eyes.

"Call me," she said, and instantly regretted it.

"Oh, I think you can count on that."

Chapter Thirteen

Sam sat in his car across the street, watching with fascination the scene before him. *A fuckin' limo,* he thought. *She's dating a guy in a fuckin' limo.*

He stared, barely peeking above the steering wheel, as the man helped Suzanne from the car. He held his arm protectively around her waist as they strolled up the walk.

"What are you goin' do now, fuck her?" he murmured darkly. He felt his anger rising. *That's MY wife!* He expected Suzanne to invite him in, the slut, but they paused at the doorway to kiss. The man ran his hand up alongside her leg, pushing the dress up to show a lot of thigh. In the dim light, he thought for a split-second that she wasn't wearing panties.

No way, man. No way. She knows better than to let it all hang out. I must be seeing things. His mind flopped about, like a fish on a dock, moving from one thought to another. *Maybe he's making her into his slut. Rich man and all.*

They kissed deeply. Sam held his anger in check. *Gotta have a plan, man, gotta have a plan.*

The boyfriend might be one avenue to explore, he mused. *Something could be done about him. Then again, he's rich—maybe there could be something in this for me.*

The man left Suzanne and headed back to his fancy-as-shit limo. Sam started the car and slipped it into gear. When the limo pulled away, he followed it.

*****

Suzanne punched the button to her answering machine as she stripped off her clothes. With a sudden start, she realized she had left her panties in Brian's limo. *I hope the driver won't find them later!* she thought, then laughed at herself.

"Hi, Suze. This is me," Wendy's voice on the tape interrupted her thoughts. "It's about eleven, I'm out with Jerry—he called me on the spur of the moment. I probably won't be home tonight. I just wanted to see how'ya doing. You sounded like you were having a great time. Of course, you may be listening to this in the morning yourself!" She cackled as she hung up.

Suzanne checked her watch. Midnight. A rather decent hour, if she did say so herself. She decided not to try Wendy on her cell phone—god only knew what she was up to right about now. She did that once and Wendy told her, "Don't bother me, I'm walking on the ceiling." When she'd said that, Suzanne had no idea what she meant until Wendy explained it to her the next day—it's when you have your legs pointed straight up while the man fucks your brains out.

God, how could she even answer her phone at a time like that?

Suzanne envied her. Not only her good looks but her success in attracting men. Sure, few were "keepers", but when she wanted to get laid, she could, regardless of how she might have felt about their long-term suitability.

Why didn't Brian want to make love to me? Is he being circumspect with all the women? Or doesn't he like me?

She put on her nightshirt, removed her makeup, brushed her teeth and then went to bed. There, lying in the dark, she thought about Brian and how he made her feel. Clearly, he liked being around a woman who thought going without underwear was earthy good fun. The thought made her loins twitch anew.

She kept Brian's face in her mind's eye as she reached down and felt along the wet slit of flesh between her legs. The "little man in the boat" was awake and alert. She rubbed the pearly nubbin with her middle finger and allowed the sensations to roll over her. She imagined Brian holding her, kissing her, stripping off his shirt to reveal that powerful chest. She wanted to run her fingers along his arms, his pecs, the flatness of his stomach…and other places as well.

Suzanne hoped that he would want to make love to her soon, perhaps by their second date. Should she play hard to get? Her body told her "no way, girl". As she stroked herself, she wondered what his penis would look like. Would it be small and of little consequence in their lovemaking—a source of frustration that money couldn't conquer? Or would it be large and hard, filling her up, making her feel like a woman? She pictured him over her, his well-toned body moving with each thrust, her hands gripping his upper arms, her legs wide as he pumped his fat, rock-hard cock deep into her again and again and again…

Suzanne wanted him. She hadn't felt like this about anybody for a long time. She wished he had come in, had grabbed her, possessed her, made her his own. Her fingers strummed her clit harder now, imagining what it would be like when Brian made love to her.

She groaned as she came, the blush spreading up from her chest to her face. Suzanne lay there, breathing heavily, thinking about Brian and how it might be when they finally made love. She laid there, her legs splayed out, her dream fading into sleep.

The next morning, Suzanne woke up feeling better than she had in months. *No wonder,* she mused, remembering the date and the effect it had on her masturbatory fantasies. She rose and debated whether she should go for a quick run or bag it and make coffee and take a warm shower. The coffee and shower won.

A few minutes later, she sat inhaling the odor of the rich roast and turning over possibilities in her mind. One, he'd call, they'd go out again, she wouldn't wear underwear as promised and it would drive him mad. He'd make love to her, perhaps in the back of his limo. She'd pretend to resist him, then give in to his manliness. She remembered his bold action when they kissed goodnight. Suzanne could still visualize his hot fingers on her upper thigh. She shuddered with need.

Down, girl.

Two, they'd go out, but the magic would be gone for some reason, and he'd drop her off early, never to call her again. Or three, they'd go out, have a great time, but he wouldn't make moves on her. Later, she'd find out he preferred another woman. He was just being polite.

Four, he wouldn't call again. She would remain an also-ran.

Her intuition told her what it would be. He wanted her. Now the question was, how did she really feel about him? Was she being swayed because he's rich? *Who wouldn't?* Did she like him? *Of course.* And finally, what would Wendy say?

She could hear her friend's voice now. *Duh. Fuck him. And I mean literally, not figuratively. Then work out the details.*

The phone rang. She knew who it was.

"Suze! How'd it go?" Wendy's voice was breathless on the line.

"Wait—you first. How'd your date with Jerry go?"

"Oh, that old story? Hell, what can I tell you? I went to his place, we took off our clothes, his dick was the size of a Louisville slugger, yada, yada, yada, I came twice. Now, your turn. Spill your guts, girl."

Suzanne filled her in. Wendy gave the appropriate "oohs" and "aahs" at the right moments, but when Suzanne got to the part about her underwear, Wendy shrieked.

"Oh, my God, girl! I can't believe you did that! I'm so proud of you! My advice is finally paying off."

"What makes you think you influenced my decision?" Suzanne said, half-teasingly.

"I'm sure I rubbed off on you a little bit—God knows I've tried to teach you how to have a good time. You were such a nun when I met you!"

"Wen, I was fourteen when you met me!"

"Yeah, well, then and now. You've hardly gotten laid in your life. It's about time."

"So you think I should go for it next time—if there is a next time."

"Oh, trust me, Suze, if you wiggled your naked ass at him, there'll be a next time."

"Wen! It wasn't like that! I had a near knee-length dress on!" She hadn't told her friend about the goodnight feel-up.

"Come on, I know men. And his mind was working overtime."

"You really think so?"

"Honey, I know so. He probably went home and choked the chicken, just thinking about you."

"Wendy Anne Thomason!" Suzanne felt her face flush at the thought. "I swear. You are the crudest woman!"

"You don't think he did? Hell, I'll bet *you* did too!"

She sputtered and she knew Wendy could tell the truth. "Oh, Suze, you're still fighting it, aren't you? Get with it—this is the twenty-first century!"

Suzanne bit her lip. "Wendy—I'm scared."

"Scared? What—that he won't call you?"

"Yeah, or that he'll like someone else better. I really like him and it's hard not to put too much hope into this relationship."

Wendy's voice softened. "I know. But you'll knock 'im dead." She paused. "Of course, we can pretty much *guarantee* you'll knock him dead."

Suzanne wasn't sure she liked the sound of that. "What are you getting at, Wen? I don't like the tone of your voice."

"It's up to you, of course. But you said yourself you're up against some tough competition. What's he have, nine women to choose from? Well, you'll probably come out on top just because of your natural good heart, don't cha think?"

Suzanne had a sinking feeling. Wendy was zeroing in on her private doubts. Her friend could play her like a fiddle.

"Okay, what do you suggest? I'm only promising to listen, you understand."

As Wendy began talking, Suzanne's eyes grew wide. "What!? You're kidding me!" Her face reddened. "Where did you get a crazy idea like that?"

She could almost hear Wendy's shrug over the phone line. "I saw it on 'Sex and the City.' But hey, it's up to you. Like I said, I'm sure you'll be first choice anyway. You probably don't have to do a *thing* to help it along."

Dammit, Wendy!

"What makes you think, um, that will work?"

"Trust me, girl, I know men. And any man who wants you to 'go commando' is gonna appreciate the little extra effort. All you're doing is just standing out a little from the crowd. Think of it as a memory aid for Brian."

Suzanne laughed and said she had to go, but really she just wanted to be alone to think about her situation. Up to now, she had been content to just drift along, only half-serious about the whole "kept woman" idea—until last night. Going out with Brian, feeling his eyes on her, basking in the warmth of his strong personality, she believed she had a connection with him. Now she wasn't sure if she could just sit by and let fate take its course. She didn't know any of the other women, but she imagined them as more beautiful, more cultured, more graceful than she.

So, what would it take to capture Brian's heart?

Chapter Fourteen

Sam stared, not believing his eyes, as he watched the man he now knew as Brian Armstrong escorting a different woman to the limousine.

"Shitfire! That's four so far! What's up with this guy?" He spoke aloud, enjoying the sound of his own voice. He had hardly spoken in jail. Now he was making up for it. He lit another cigarette from the butt in his mouth and tossed the dead one out the window.

Since he'd started following Armstrong, Sam had gotten a glimpse at how rich people live. Every day, his driver would pick him up at his ritzy townhouse and drive him to a glittering office building downtown. The car's license plate had led him to Armstrong Control Systems and a check of the web page turned up a nice color picture of the man who turned out to be the fuckin' CEO.

That surprise paled when Sam started following Armstrong when he went out at night. In a week, he'd been seen with three other women, all very good-looking. Just like his Suzanne.

How'd I ever let her slip away? he thought, then flashed on her sitting in the courtroom when he was sentenced, smirking at him. *Oh, yes, I remember. The bitch. Don't worry, I'll get even with you soon.*

Sam followed the limo to Chinatown. He knew they were heading to a restaurant—*that's all this guy seems to do is eat. It's a wonder he isn't as fat as Marlon Brando.* Again, just as he'd done all the other times Sam had followed the limo, the driver pulled into a side street to let his passengers off rather than double-park in traffic. When Sam pulled up to the side street, he could see Armstrong and the leggy blonde heading toward him. He drove off smoothly, sure they didn't know he'd been spying on them.

He watched in his rearview mirror as they walked to a Chinese restaurant and went inside.

Same pattern, he thought. Armstrong took each cunt to an ethnic restaurant and sometimes they weren't in the best parts of town. What's he doing, slumming? Guy like that could afford the Excelsior Club. And why is he going out with so many broads? Of course, Sam knew he shouldn't be surprised. Hell, if he were rich, he'd have women all over him too. Bitches seem to flock to money.

And all the dates lately seemed to be the same. After he took them to a small restaurant, they'd go out dancing. Woman ate that shit up, you bet.

So, does that mean that he's going to be seeing Suzanne again? And if he does, will she get the same treatment? For that matter, does she know about all the other cunts? Maybe he could make an anonymous call, telling her what a rat her lover was. Of course, she'd recognize his voice right away, so that wouldn't work. He'd have to get someone to do it. He mentally shrugged. Heck, she might not care about the others. She's probably busting her hump to land this Armstrong herself. Who wouldn't?

A germ of an idea began forming in his head. It wasn't the main idea, far from it. That he would have to think on some more. But it was a nice little idea and he nurtured it.

A way to take this asshole down a peg or two in front of Suzie.

A good fuckin' start, he told himself. *A start on payback for all the months I spent locked up while you peddled your ass all over town.*

* * * * *

Brian smiled at Carol as she sat across from him in the restaurant. Before he could speak, Lo Ming, his favorite waitress, approached.

"Good evening, Mr. Armstrong," she said, bowing slightly. She turned to Carol. "Ma'am. Can I get you anything from the bar?"

"Yes, I'll have a martini…and what would you like?" he asked his date.

"Um, do you have rum and Coke?"

Brian tried not to shudder as he gave the order. Lo Ming bowed again and disappeared.

"So, I imagine you're curious about me. Is there anything you'd like to ask me?" Brian looked her over. She was a tall, delicate woman. Her blonde hair framed her face, coming down just to her shoulders. She seemed perfectly made-up, a living doll.

"Uh, well." She seemed nervous. "Do you come here often?"

"You mean, this restaurant? Yes, quite a bit. It's not that far from my office and the food is very good."

She nodded absently, her eyes darting around. Brian wondered if she'd run out of things to say already.

"Do you like Chinese food?"

"Um, I don't eat it much. Mostly just American food." She smiled briefly.

"Would you rather go somewhere else?"

"Oh, no! This is fine. Just fine."

Lo Ming came back with the drinks, then immediately left again.

Carol sat up. "She forgot to give us menus. How rude!"

"Actually," Brian put in. "I took the liberty of ordering for you when I made the reservation."

She glanced up sharply. "How'dya know what I like?" She seemed offended.

Brian was taken aback. "Um. I just guessed, from what I know about you. Was that all right?"

Carol seemed to catch herself. "Oh. Um, sure. What is it going to be?"

He almost said, "It's a surprise," then caught himself. Carol didn't seem like the surprise type. She must be hell on Christmas, he thought.

"Peking duck for two. It's their specialty. Do you like duck?"

"I don't know. I haven't had it before. It'll probably be all right. But I like to order my own dinners, usually." She took a long pull on her drink.

Brian tried to break through the wall she had suddenly put up. She had been far more relaxed during the video session. "You seem nervous. Are you uncomfortable here with me?"

"No, no. I'm… It's just that I haven't been out on such a mysterious date before. You know, all this secrecy, the questions…"

"Why did you do it, then? Why not just tell Rebecca that you'd just as soon forget it?"

"I really wanted to meet you. You know, find out what the CEO of a large company is really like and all. But you seem like a regular guy."

Brian knew in that instant that Carol was more interested in dating his wallet than him. He tried not to show his impatience as he took a sip of his drink.

"Do you date many, um, CEOs?" He meant that as a euphemism for rich men.

"Not CEOs, per se, but, you know, men like you."

Carol was a gold-digger. "I imagine you enjoy that lifestyle."

"Well, of course! Who wouldn't?"

Time seemed to crawl after that moment, Brian reflected later.

Chapter Fifteen

Brian didn't call Suzanne for more than a week. Halloween loomed and the grinning pumpkins she saw everywhere mocked her. More than once she told Wendy that she was sure he'd never call. But Wendy pointed out that Suzanne had been told she was Brian's fifth date, out of nine.

"Do the math, girl," she had said over a glass of wine ten days later. "He went out with you Friday. He probably had another one lined up Saturday, and then with work and all, he waited until the following weekend to date the last two. Right?"

Suzanne thought she made sense. Dare she hope?

As if by magic, Brian called the very next night. Suzanne was alone, thankfully. She didn't know if she'd be able to talk coherently with Wendy giggling in the background.

"Brian! How nice to hear from you again." She hoped she sounded cool. She didn't want him to hear her sigh of relief.

"I had a good time on our date. I was hoping you'd like to go out with me again."

"Well, yes. I would, very much. I was wondering if you'd want to collect on our bet." A flush of embarrassment flashed through her. Normally, she wouldn't have mentioned the bet, but Wendy had insisted.

"You gotta meet him halfway, girl. Show him you're really interested," she had told her.

She heard him chuckle. "Yes, I'm glad you remembered. I like it when you go 'commando' style."

He was being polite, yet Suzanne could hear the strength in his voice. This man liked to be in control and she enjoyed letting him. She instinctively wanted to trust him. She wanted to hear him talk dirty to her, tell her what he wanted to do to her in graphic terms. She pressed the flat of her hand against her mound through her jeans and bit her lip to keep from groaning aloud.

"Um, I'm really glad you called, Brian. I was worried you'd chosen another, uh, contestant."

"It does feel like a game show, doesn't it?" He sounded a little embarrassed.

"No, it's all right. I'm just glad you wanted to go out again."

"I did beat you fair and square, didn't I?" he teased her.

She laughed, another real laugh. "Yes, you did. So what do you have in mind?" She touched herself again, just briefly, thrilled with the idea that maybe he might make love to her.

"Let's let it be a surprise, shall we?"

Oh, does this man like surprises. She thought again of what Wendy had told her. "Very well. I'm game." *And I'll have a surprise for you,* she thought—but only if things progress to a certain point. Did she want them to?

* * * * *

He had arranged to pick her up in the limo Friday night. Suzanne paid careful attention to detail as she got ready. This time, she needed Wendy's help. When she came out of the bathroom after her shower, still dressed in her robe, Wendy crossed her arms and cocked her head.

"Well? Did you?"

"I don't know how you talked me into this Wen. He's gonna laugh his head off."

"It's just a lark. A gag. It will make you stand out. Isn't that the point? Don't make it into a big deal."

"I'm trying to keep it in perspective. It just feels weird."

"Well?" she said again, wiggling her fingers at Suzanne's robe in a "come on" fashion.

"I'm too embarrassed."

"Suze, I've seen you naked. Don't worry, I'm not bi."

Sighing, Suzanne opened her robe. Wendy shrieked and clapped her hands. There, where Suzanne's triangular brown bush had been, was a finely sculpted little lightning bolt, the point ending just above her clitoris.

She closed her robe fast, like she was performing a karate move. "He's going to think I'm such a freak."

Wendy, wiping tears from her eyes, said, "No way. I'm telling you, hon, he is going to be putty in your hands. Men love it when women prepare themselves like this."

"You make it sound like we're planning an invasion."

"No, Suze, it's much more subtle. Not an invasion, more like a 'commando' raid." She giggled at her own pun. "We're going in to take the enemy's headquarters!"

"He's not the enemy!"

"I know, I know." Wendy waved her hand dismissively. "Just a figure of speech. But the analogy is apt—by the time we're done, he won't know what hit him. He'll just have to surrender."

"He's not like that," Suzanne insisted. She didn't think Wendy would understand—she could never submit to a man like Brian. Wendy loved to be in control too much.

Suzanne suddenly felt inadequate. "Oh, Wen, do you really think I have a chance?"

"Now you stop that negative thinking. He obviously likes you, and when he sees you tonight, he's gonna flip."

He's going to see me – the question is, how much of me?

Suzanne returned to the bedroom, Wendy close behind. She had laid out her outfit for the evening, a sleeveless, dark blue dress dotted in white. Large buttons ran down the front. After showing off her artistry with the razor, Suzanne felt self-conscious so she retired to the bathroom to slip into her outfit. She left the door ajar so they could talk. She dropped the robe and took one last look at herself in the full-length mirror. *Damn! I look pretty good,* she told herself. Breasts still firm, slender hips with just a little bit of extra padding and long legs that were ready to wrap around a good man. Only the silly lightning bolt seemed jarring. She had a sudden urge to shave it off but decided to go with Wendy's suggestion for now. After all, she was an expert on men. Wasn't she?

Now, as she buttoned the dress up the front, the idea that she'd be naked underneath all evening made her feel sexy and wanton.

"Um, I've been meaning to ask you something, Wen," she called out. "What if he, you know, makes his move on me? Do you think I should give in or hold out?" Her heart and her pussy said give in, while her head remained more practical.

"Well, you know what I would do," Wendy replied. "A rich guy like that? I'd be walking on the ceiling the first night, even if I had to strip naked in the limo to get him in the mood. But I know you are one of the last good girls left on Earth, so we have to protect you. Wouldn't do to have you sacrifice your virginity on the altar of passion, now would it?"

Suzanne finished the last button and returned to the bed to pick up her necklace. "I'm not a virgin! You know that."

"Really? The way I hear, if it goes unused for a certain period of time, it grows back."

Suzanne tossed a pillow at her. "Now, come on, I'm serious. I know what you would do. But this is me we're talking about. Do you think it would help me or hurt me—you know, in the long run?"

Wendy sighed. "Oh, Suze, you are such a Girl Scout. I'd say play it by ear—but if he acts interested, go for it. I'll bet you the other 'contestants' are doing the same thing."

Suzanne grimaced. "I'm not sure I like the thought of that."

"What? That's he getting laid? Grow up, girl—men would get laid every day if they could."

"Yeah, but the idea of him sharing himself with so many others—I-I might catch something."

Wendy took both of her friend's hands in hers. "You *do* have a condom in your purse, don't you?"

Suzanne hadn't thought about it before. "Er, no, I don't. Should I have?" She thought men were in charge of such things.

Wendy just shook her head and began fishing into her purse. "What would you do without me?" She pulled out a foil-wrapped package. "Here. It's on me. Next time, buy a three-pack and keep them handy. Men don't always plan ahead. Remember, men are pigs. Brian excepted, of course."

Suzanne nodded and took the package gratefully. "Okay, I'm a Girl Scout. And now I'm prepared."

The doorbell rang.

Chapter Sixteen

Sam turned to the two men in his car. "There they are."

"It's about fuckin' time," the small man said from the backseat. "Seems like we been ridin' around with you for days." The big man in the front seat said nothing, just stared straight ahead.

"Relax, Jarvis. You're being paid, aren't cha? The guy dates so many broads, it's hard to keep up. My wife is the only one I'm interested in."

"That's your ex? She's got a hot bod."

Sam turned and glared at Jarvis. "Shut your mouth."

Jarvis held up both hands, palms out. "Hey, relax. I was just payin' her a compliment."

Sam pulled into traffic two cars back of the limo. "You guys know what to do?"

"Yeah, yeah, we rough up the rich guy, make him look like a chump in front of the *la-dy*." He said the last word with emphasis, like he was talking about a delicate work of art. "But we don't kill him or nuthin'. And anythin' we get off of Daddy Warbucks, we keep."

"Yeah. And keep your hands off the cunt. She's mine." He grabbed the big man's meaty bicep. "You got that, Mack?"

The big man's head swiveled slowly toward him. "I don't beat up women," he said, his voice a rumble. Sam felt vaguely threatened so he dropped his hand.

"Good. I'm gonna see where they're going and drop you off when they pull into a side street. You make sure the limo takes off, and then go into your bit. I'll circle the block and pick you up on the next street."

Jarvis leaned forward. "Don't try to stiff us on the back end. You still owe us five bills."

Sam had no intention of stiffing them. He'd hidden away three thousand dollars from Suzanne during the divorce. This and the gun would be the perfect use for it. "Relax. You'll probably make twice that off Armstrong. You know he's a big hotshot C-E-fuckin'-O. Prolly has lots of cash."

Sam was pleased to see they were entering a working-class neighborhood. "Slumming again, fuck-face?" he mused.

"What's that?" Jarvis said sharply.

"Just talkin' to myself. You see this guy? He's so predictable. He's taking every one of his broads to some crappy restaurant. It's like a fuckin' assembly line."

He noticed the limo's right blinker went on. "This is it, guys."

* * * * *

Suzanne grabbed Brian's upper arm and tried not to scream. Two men had come out of the shadows, blocking their path to the street. One was large, maybe a football player gone to seed. His eyes were black and mean, about the size of watermelon seeds. His hair was cropped close to his head. He had a scar that ran from just below his left eye through the top of his ear, truncating the appendage like a flattop haircut.

The other man was smaller and jittery, like he'd just drunk six cups of coffee. Suzanne suspected he had taken something stronger than that. His eyes were round and shiny like quarters and the corner of his mouth twitched when he eyed her. He made her feel naked. She cringed, wishing she had worn underwear all of a sudden. And maybe a suit of armor.

While the big man stayed in front, the smaller man moved to Brian's left side. With the edge of the building to their right, they had only one escape route left—behind them, down the street away from the traffic and further into the darkness. Suzanne knew she couldn't run as fast as the small man, especially in high heels and a tight dress. She mentally prepared to kick her shoes off, hike her dress up and sprint, waiting only for Brian to move. But he remained strangely quiet, making no effort to get away.

"Got the time?" the smaller man said. He looked like a rodent.

Brian eyed the man flatly. Suzanne could see the curve of his face. The strong jaw, clenching now under his cheek. He didn't seem scared—that surprised her. She was terrified.

"I'd say about eight," Brian replied, without looking at his watch. His voice sounded unnaturally calm. Suzanne thought she might pee herself.

This was going to be an important date! How could this be happening? They had hit it off so well last time, and she had been thrilled to be asked out again tonight. She and Wendy had planned her outfit so carefully. It was to be a fun, sexy, interesting evening. Now this!

She anticipated that their conversation would become more intimate over tonight's meal. Brian said he had chosen a "very special place" to take her. A family restaurant he'd been patronizing much of his life, he told her. "Best Italian food in the city," he had promised.

In retrospect, Suzanne should've been more concerned about the location. Rico's Italian Restaurant sat on a block that probably had been respectable twenty years ago but now seemed marginal. As they had glided through in the limo, Suzanne had seen a knot of men, both black and white, hanging outside a carry-out just two doors down from the restaurant. Somewhere a car stereo had boomed loudly.

Suzanne hadn't really been concerned—after all, it was still early in the evening. There was plenty of foot traffic. Except for this one short stretch of block where Baba had stopped the limo, just around the corner from the restaurant. Brian had told him not to wait so Baba had driven off.

The men must've been waiting for someone to rob and she and Brian had walked right into their trap. Suzanne could see the brighter lights of the cross street less than a half-block down, past the massive shoulder of the brutish man.

She stood there, grasping Brian's arm, feeling his muscles move under his shirt and thought her life might change forever in the next few minutes. She wanted to run—she wanted to cry.

The smaller man didn't seem to like Brian's answer. He probably had wanted a glimpse of Brian's watch, to gauge how rich their victims were.

"Okay," he snarled, pulling a small, silver gun from his jacket, "Give me your wallet, asshole. The watch, too."

Brian just stood there, staring at the man. Suzanne had expected quite a different reaction. Perhaps Brian would show great fear. Perhaps he would beg for their lives.

Instead, he became unnaturally calm. It was as if the breeze had stopped blowing around them. Her dad would've called it Earthquake Weather—that sudden stillness that proceeds some cataclysmic event.

Suzanne felt Brian drop his right arm down and press the flat of his hand against her hip. His thumb actually touched her mound, sending a shiver through her, although it wasn't a sexual act. She understood his meaning and allowed herself to be pushed back, out of harm's way, closer to the wall.

"We don't want any trouble," Brian was saying. He used victim's words, but in that odd flat tone. Although Suzanne didn't know him all that well yet, it seemed false somehow.

"Just do what you're told and no one gets hurt," the smaller man said. "The wallet first."

Brian nodded in response. "Okay, my wallet is in my inside coat pocket. I'm getting it now. Please don't hurt us." She saw him glance over at the big man, who stood like a statue.

Suzanne's heart beat rapidly and she felt short of breath. She watched as Brian stepped forward and turned slightly, so the gunman could see him reach in for his wallet. He did so with careful exaggeration, even opening his sport coat with his right to show he had no weapons.

Brian held it out with his left hand. The crook grinned at his larger partner and reached out with his left hand to take it, his gun steady in his right fist.

That's when all hell broke loose.

As Brian spoke to the smaller man, he tried to play the part of a victim as best he could. He knew if he acted arrogant or indignant, they'd probably be shot by this twitchy man. He tried to keep his body loose as he held out the wallet.

He glanced at the larger thug, but he seemed content to stand placidly, blocking their escape. He had the appearance of an ex-boxer. He reminded Brian of a good ol' Southern boy he used to know named Bubba. Big and dumb, but strong, like the character in *Of Mice and Men. Tell me about the rabbits, George!* Brian knew he may seem harmless, but underneath he probably itched to pummel somebody.

Brian concentrated his attention on the smaller man, the one with sharp features and a large nose, like a rat. Ratman was about three inches shorter than he was, he guessed, and probably weighed about forty pounds less. Not much of an edge, considering the gun pointed at his midsection, but it would have to do. He was just glad it wasn't the larger man with the gun. He wondered if the big guy had a gun as well, tucked out of sight. He had to assume he did.

When Ratman reached out for the wallet with his left hand, his gun hand naturally drifted to the right, taking it offline from the center of Brian's body. He reacted instantly.

He dropped the wallet just before Ratman grabbed it and swiveled his hand down to slap the gun away. There was a sharp report as the gun discharged harmlessly to the left, ricocheting off the cinderblock wall. To his right, he heard Suzanne give a yelp of surprise and shock. For a moment, he feared she'd been shot. Brian grabbed the cylinder of the weapon, snap-kicked Ratman to the groin, planted his foot and punched him straight into his nose.

The kick had propelled Ratman's face forward, meeting Brian's fist. The crunching sound and his high-pitched scream came at the same time. Brian yanked the gun free of his slackening hand and dipped down, driving his left shoulder into the smaller man. Ratman fell back and sprawled in the alley.

Bubba's eyes widened and he reached out to grab Brian's shoulder, his right arm cocked for a deadly blow. Brian stepped right inside the big man's grasp, chest to chest, making it impossible for the man to punch him. As Brian moved, he slapped the butt of the gun into his right hand. The larger man pulled Brian to him in a bear hug, ready to crush the life from him, only to feel the cold hard edge of the barrel pressed tightly against the underside of his jaw. His pig-eyes grew large.

"Let go and step back or I'll put a couple o' rounds into your skull," Brian growled. Bubba let go and held up both hands, and backed off. Brian could see him taking in the scene—his friend, writhing on the ground, blood running out from between his fingers pressed to his face, the cold-eyed stranger before him, holding the gun. Bubba took another step back, then circled left around behind Ratman and ran, leaving his partner behind.

When Ratman saw he'd been abandoned, he rolled to his feet and staggered off after him, daring Brian to shoot him.

Brian didn't.

He turned to Suzanne. "Are you all right?" He put his arm around her. Suzanne nodded, the fear seeping out of her bones like water squeezed from a sponge.

"Well, that kinda put a damper on the evening, huh?" He gazed at the gun in his hand then tossed it into a nearby trashcan. "I'm really sorry about all that. Let's get out of here, okay?" He pulled out his cell phone.

Chapter Seventeen

Suzanne, watching Brian dialing his cell phone, didn't know what to think. She had been so afraid a moment ago, fearing she'd be raped or worse. Yet now, when the danger had passed, she felt exhilarated. Giddy, almost. Moreover, she feared how she handled this moment would reflect on what kind of woman she was.

"No," she said before Brian could dial Baba's number. "No, you wanted to show me this great restaurant. Let's not let a couple of punks ruin our evening."

Brian raised his eyebrows, the phone still at half-mast in his left hand. "You sure you don't want to call the cops, file a report?"

"What good would it do? Besides, we'd be at the station half the night, answering questions or looking at mug books. I'm hungry." *Truth is, I want you to fuck me.* Her own thoughts startled her. She considered herself to be a good girl, yet the sight of Brian taking on those thugs had excited her no end. She wanted to be taken by him.

Brian nodded slowly and put the phone away. "If you're not too freaked out. This is a great restaurant and it's run by some family friends. They're looking forward to meeting you."

"How many others have you taken here?" Suzanne regretted the words as soon as they were out of her mouth. "I'm sorry. I didn't mean to pry."

"No, it's all right." He put his arm around her waist and began to escort her up the street. "You're the first one I've taken here. Some of the others would never be caught dead in this neighborhood." He winced at his poor choice of words.

* * * * *

Sam couldn't believe his eyes. Mack came toward his car, holding up Jarvis, who had blood running down through his fingers that he held to his face.

When they neared, Sam could tell Jarvis was furious. He cursed a blue streak, angry at Mack, Armstrong—even Sam. Mack piled Jarvis into the backseat and got in front. Sam drove off, his eyes darting from the passenger seat to the rearview mirror to traffic ahead.

"Fuckin' guy!" Jarvis talked through his hand. "You just stood dere like some kinda statue! I'm doin' all the work—you did shit!" Mack turned around to stare at him, eyes narrowed. Jarvis seemed to sense he was going too far. "And you," he turned his fury on Sam. "You shudda warned me! You said it was an easy job. A quick five hunner!" He took the tissues Sam handed him and plugged up his nose. "Now lokka me! He bro' my dose!"

"What the hell happened?" Sam asked Mack.

Mack shrugged. "He got the drop on Jarvis."

Sam sat back, stunned. That this rich fuck had any balls had never occurred to him. He turned half around to Jarvis. "I thought you had a gun?"

"I di', I di'! He di' som' fancy shi' and toog it away."

Sam was incredulous. "He took it away?"

"Karate," Mack put in. "He moved pretty fast."

"Yeah, fash! Du jus' 'tood dere!"

"He took Jarvis' gun and held it to my neck. I couldn't punch him."

"So you got nuthin'? What about the girl? She okay?"

Mack nodded. "She's fine."

"Du owe be mo' money!" Jarvis said from the backseat. "I dever agree' to git by dose broke!"

Sam didn't want to get into an argument with these useless jerk-offs. "Five hundred each—that's what we agreed on. You want more, you can take it out of Mack's share."

The backseat grew suddenly quiet.

*****

Despite the scare, the dinner went very well. They talked, they laughed, they shared bites from each other's plates. She met the owners, Rico and Sophia, who fussed over her and made her feel at home. The food, as had been promised, was excellent. Fresh pasta, made with an unusual mix of flavors, and rich, red wine made the meal complete. Suzanne sat back, satisfied. The ugly incident from earlier that evening was already fading from her mind.

"Thanks," she said. "That was really good."

"Worth the near-death experience?"

"I don't know about that," she said truthfully. "But for some reason, it did make me hungrier."

And hornier.

As Sophia served them coffee, Suzanne reached out and touched his hand. "So, what's next? Bullfighting? Dessert in Beirut? Running with the bulls?" Too many bull references, she realized. Perhaps she was speculating on the size of Brian's cock.

Down, girl! She shifted in her seat, suddenly a little antsy. She had almost forgotten about her lack of underwear, but now felt vulnerable, in a naughty kind of way.

"Well, I was going to take you dancing. I don't know about you, but I'm a little shaky still. How about a walk along the Embarcadero instead?"

"Will there be bodyguards?" she teased.

"Do you need them for potential robbers or for me?" he shot back.

A grin danced over Suzanne's face. "I have no doubt now that you could take care of any thugs…" She let the sentence hang unfinished, thinking, *No, I don't need any protection from you. I'm open and ready.*

She visualized being taken by this graceful and powerful man. He could hold her with one arm and easily have his way with her. The image burst forth full-flowered. Her body being held gently but firmly up against a stone railing. The sound of the waves below. The smell of the sea. His insistent hand pulling at her dress, unbuttoning it feverishly from below as if his blood was up. Suzanne would play coy, pushing ineffectually at his broad chest with one hand and making mild protests, while her free hand would be at his belt, unfastening his pants.

Her nipples would be hard, pressing almost painfully against the material of her dress. Brian would reach in, feeling the expanse of bare flesh along her thighs. Her skin would be hot, her pussy wet and swollen with need.

Her fingers would close around his cock, causing her to gasp at its size and rigidity. His hand would come up for a moment to unbutton her dress and caress her breast before returning to prepare her. As she freed him from his pants, he would press her legs apart. She would willingly help him, easing herself up onto the broad railing, her head thrown back. Her hand would steer his cock toward her—

"Suzanne?"

Suzanne came back to reality, her face flushed. "Um. Yes?"

"You seemed to drift off there for a moment. Are you all right?"

"Oh, yes. Yes." Her blush deepened. It was as if her thoughts had spilled out on the table for all to see. She wondered if Brian was having similar thoughts. Suddenly, she felt naked. She glanced around the nearly deserted restaurant. Was everyone looking at her or did it only feel that way?

"Are you ready to go?"

No, I'm ready to come.

"Yes, yes." She stood. "Let me visit the ladies' room." She excused herself before Brian could rise fully to his feet. She closed the door behind her and shut her eyes a moment, breathing deeply. She peeked around and was grateful to be alone. In the mirror, she could see the red flush in her cheekbones. Her eyes seemed overly bright.

"What's the matter with you, you horny slut?" she whispered to her reflection. Quickly, she wet a paper towel and daubed at her neck, trying to cool her ardor. She wanted to dip her face into a bucket of ice water, but didn't want to ruin her makeup.

Suzanne went into a stall and hiked up her dress. Her pussy oozed with lubrication, she made a face. Taking a wad of toilet paper, she cleaned up as best she could. She had never felt this attracted to a man before. It was as if her body had a mind of its own.

Maybe this is how men feel all the time, she thought, then giggled.

Straightening up, she checked her image one more time and reapplied her lipstick. Finally, squaring her shoulders, Suzanne marched herself out of the bathroom and into the next stage of her adventure.

Chapter Eighteen

Brian thought Suzanne seemed a bit flustered and attributed it to the attack. He cursed himself for picking that restaurant, even if it was one his favorites. He made sure she felt safe at the ocean—he directed Baba to drive them to the well-populated park along the Embarcadero. Many couples walked along the path, including an occasional cop.

They strolled along, hand-in-hand, like two old friends. Brian thought her skin felt hot, as if she had a slight fever. The wind carried the first chill of autumn. He offered Suzanne his dinner jacket, which she accepted gratefully.

As he draped it over her shoulders, he imagined her hot flesh underneath her dress, her breasts swinging free. This led to other images—her mouth opened in pleasure, her fingers digging into his shoulders, her legs wrapped around him. Now that he was with her, he felt a bit ashamed about imaging her to be a subservient slave—yet he couldn't dismiss the thought. His cock swelled as he recalled beating off to her image the other day.

He shook his head. *Go slow, mister! You don't know if she's the one!*

"Are you all right? Are you cold?" Suzanne tugged on his hand to bring him around to face her.

"I'm fine. Just fine. Why do you ask?"

"You seemed to shudder there for just a minute."

"Oh, it was nothing." He couldn't think of a plausible answer to give her. He didn't want to bring up the robbery attempt. But he certainly didn't want to tell her he just imagined them fucking like rabbits. He feared he might scare her off. "Maybe I am cold."

Suzanne looked at him speculatively, as if she didn't believe him. "Do you want your jacket back?"

"No, I'm fine. Let's walk." He put his arm around her and they strolled together.

"I had a good time, um, despite…the excitement."

"Good. I'm glad to hear that. I was worried…you know…"

"It wasn't your fault. You sure took care of them quickly. Made me feel very safe."

He nodded. He longed to tell her how she made him feel. "Would you like to go out with me again?"

"Sure," she said brightly. "I'd like that."

"Not a restaurant this time. Someplace far away from any bad neighborhoods." He wrestled with how to suggest his next step. Would she be shocked?

She paused, and leaned back against the stone railing. Brian watched her run her hand along the expanse of block. She spread her legs slightly and hiked one thigh up on the stone surface. He wondered what she was thinking.

"What then? More miniature golf?" She teased him and he liked it. His mind remained centered on her dress, pulled tight along her thighs. He fought to keep from staring at the straining buttons. God how he wanted her!

"No, I have something really special planned."

"Oh, I bet you say that to all your girls." She was fishing now, he could tell.

"No, if you agree to this, you'll be the first. Maybe the only one."

She looked up. Brian could see the intensity in her eyes. She didn't speak. She just waited for him to continue. For a moment, he lost his voice.

"You see, I—" He stopped, and plunged ahead. "I was wondering if you'd like to spend the weekend with me at my island. You know, the one we talked about earlier."

Will you make love to me there?

Suzanne almost said it aloud. Almost. She knew he would, eventually. Lots of lovemaking. She longed to feel this man's chest against hers, feel his arms around her, protecting her, holding her close, his hard cock entering her. She liked the sensation she received from leaning against the railing, her thighs slightly spread, the air blowing across her naked loins.

She realized Brian was staring at her, waiting for a response. Funny, she thought she'd given it. "Oh, yes, I remember. That sounds nice," she said lamely. "Off the coast?"

"Actually, no. It's on a lake. Clear Lake. Just north of here."

Suzanne wasn't sure it sounded private enough for what she had in mind—lots of naked romping. "Really? I didn't know there were too many lake islands. How big is it?"

"About fifty acres. It's very private." *He must've read my mind,* she thought.

"Sounds, um, very nice." *Tell me about the fucking.*

"I have a vacation home on it, fully equipped. Lots of trees and trails. It's like a little Eden, not very far from civilization."

"Um. Do people rent it when you're not there?"

Brian shook his head. "No. It's just for me. And my guests."

"What about Baba—or other, um, servants?"

"Nope. Just you and me. Does that scare you? Do you trust me?"

Trust you to do what? Make me walk on the ceiling? "Sure, I trust you."

"I'm glad to hear it. I don't ask every woman I meet to see it."

So, I stand out from the crowd, she thought at once. Suzanne couldn't help but smile. *This seems to be going very well. Mister, you'd better be as good in real life as you are in my imagination!*

He moved in close, putting his arms around her. Suzanne cursed her dress, realizing it was too tight across her thighs. She wanted to welcome him between her legs. She was both shocked by her behavior and relished it. *It's about time!*

He kissed her. She rose up to meet him like a baby bird, eager to partake in his warmth, his lust. Again, he kissed like a man who had had a lot of practice—not hard enough to bruise. Not like Sam. She cursed her memory for bringing that up now. Suzanne closed her eyes and tried to lose herself into this wonderful man.

His hands roamed over her body. She wished she was naked, open to his touch. No, not here. Somewhere private. The island would do very nicely. She felt his hand brush her left breast. Her nipple extended to its full length, poking into the dress. She pressed against his fingers, encouraging him. His thumb rubbed over her turgid nipple.

Brian reached down, touching her thigh, just above her knee, where the dress strained. She was lost in his embrace now. Without thinking, she eased off the wall, giving him total access to her. Just as he did the other night, Brian let his right hand pull up her dress a few inches. She was acutely embarrassed, but didn't make any attempt to stop him. If he wanted to show off her nakedness in the park, she was ready.

Suddenly, he let the dress fall back into place and pulled away, holding her at arm's length. Perhaps it had only been another test. Yet the look in his eyes told her different.

"Come on, I'll take you home." His voice was slightly hoarse. He licked his lips.

Inside the limo once again, Suzanne noticed that Brian left the privacy screen up behind the driver. She sat across from him, waiting to see what he'd do. She sat with her legs slightly askew—just enough to hint at the pleasures within. Her pussy ached with frustration. Part of her longed to hike up her skirt again, lie down on the seat and rut with him. But that still seemed more like Wendy talking. Instinctively, she knew to let Brian control the pace of their relationship.

"That last button on your dress looks like it's about to come off." His words startled her. She looked down. "Why don't you unbutton it, take the pressure off? I'd hate to have you lose it."

Suzanne dutifully unhooked it, knowing that it showed a little more of her legs. *You ain't seen nothin' yet,* she thought. "Is that better?"

"Yes," he said. He gestured. "Here, give me one of your feet. I'll bet you'd like a foot rub."

She smiled coyly. *Are you trying to peek at my private parts?* She almost let it slip. She had a feeling one day she could say such things and it would be all right. She lifted her right leg toward him, letting the dress part, revealing tanned thighs. She shifted slightly to retain her modesty, though she knew soon, very soon, she'd be showing him everything. So would he. She longed to see his cock, feel it.

He took her foot into his strong hands and began rubbing the ball, just below her toes, right where it ached the most. It was as if he read her body. Of course, he'd have to be blind not to notice that.

Brian gently stroked her foot moving up through the arch to the heel then back again. The sensation made her weak with release, gratitude and, yes, lust. Always lust. It remained thick in the air of the limo. These are the best times in any relationship, she thought, the days and hours before sex, when all your sensations hinge on the anticipation of the event.

He moved her foot to the left, as if he wanted to rub the inside of her arch, below the anklebone. Suzanne noticed at once that it caused her legs to come apart a little more, exposing more thigh. She pretended not to notice. Then Brian reached out and unfastened the second button from the bottom. Her dress opened more. She could feel cooler air on her wispy hair down there.

Her pussy throbbed. Suzanne closed her eyes. She could use a little rubdown there as well, she mused, and smiled.

"Does that feel good?"

"Oh, yeah. Great." *It's not very often that your date is not only handsome, rich and kind, but that he gives killer foot rubs as well!*

"Okay. Now the other one."

She took back her foot reluctantly and handed over the other one. This time, her dress rose up even higher, the V of the cloth barely covering her nakedness. She could smell the sweet scent of her own sex, drawing him in.

She opened her eyes and caught him looking at her face. She had expected his eyes to be elsewhere. She blushed then shot him a grateful smile. Brian turned her foot to the outside, and by now Suzanne was sure she was giving him a little show there in the darkened limo. She almost said something, and knew it would be both coy and teasing, maybe a bit sarcastic. She worried it wouldn't come across right and could kill the mood, so she said nothing.

She watched his face and he watched hers. It was as if she was daring him to let his eyes drop down to her legs. *Come on, here I am, take a peek!*

His eyes finally dropped to the V of her legs. Suzanne found herself actually widening them, inviting him to look. His eyebrow went up when he spotted her unusual design.

"Is that what I think it is?"

She smiled. "Perhaps you need a closer look." *God, did I just say that? I sound like Wendy!*

"That could lead to trouble."

"Depends on your definition of the word."

She sat up and started to pull her dress together, but he stopped her.

"Don't," he said in a soft but firm voice. "I like you like this."

"What? Exposed?"

"No. Well, yes, but I was thinking of something else." He paused, and then said, "Pliable."

Suzanne did feel pliable at that minute. And a little slutty. She'd never had a man treat her this way. It made her want him all the more.

He reached in between her legs and cupped her sex, his fingers pressing hard against her clit. With a sudden shudder, Suzanne came. She could feel her wetness covering his fingers. She wanted to touch him, to gauge his hardness. She wanted him inside her. How could he hold back?

Brian pulled his hand away, causing her to wither, like a flower cut off from sunlight. *Please, please fuck me!* If he wanted her pliable, he got his wish. She thought she might melt into the floor.

He brought his hand up and stroked his fingers along her cheek, spreading her wetness, her own scent, on her face. It seemed an act of ownership, as if he were saying, "This is mine now. You are mine."

Brian moved his fingers to her mouth and she opened up automatically, taking them in, tasting her own juices, surrendering herself to him completely. Her legs splayed open now, ready for whatever he wanted to do.

Brian eased down, pushing her dress up higher. Suzanne felt like she was someone else at that moment. *This is so unlike me! Isn't it?*

But there was something about this man that made her want to expose herself to him, give her body to him. Not just the raw attraction of him, but something more, something deeper.

She felt his warm breath on her wetness. She bit her lip. For a moment, her guilt returned, telling her good girls don't do this, good girls don't act like sluts in the back of limos. She pushed the thought aside. *This girl does.* It just felt right. She trusted Brian, even though she barely knew him. He exuded power, like the way he handled those two men. Perhaps it was a basic instinct inherent in all women. Go for the man who can defeat other men—the Alpha Male. Brian was all of that.

When his tongue touched her for the first time, Suzanne gasped. Her legs twitched and she didn't know if she wanted him to stop or go on. She needed him inside her. Yet she enjoyed the waiting too. She wanted him to control the situation, be the boss. Again, he touched her. She found herself thrusting her hips at him, making little noises in her throat.

Brian kissed her wet pussy, smearing her juices all over his lips, sucking at her hard clit and Suzanne exploded again. It happened so suddenly; it took her by surprise. She usually took a while to warm up, but not with this powerful man—a mere touch sent her off. She cried out and grasped his head tight against her in order to make him stop stimulating her for just a minute. She couldn't bear it.

She released him and he blew out a breath, and they both laughed. She wasn't done and she hoped she hadn't ruined the mood. She needn't have worried. He dipped back to her pleasure point and began again. It took longer this time, but not much longer.

"Oh, god, oh, god—Brian!"

Another wave of pleasure rocked her. She knew she was a soppy mess now, leaking all over the limo's cushions, but she didn't care. Nor did she care that the driver could probably hear her clearly. She had never abandoned herself to a man like this before. She wanted him inside her—right now!

Brian eased back and she expected him to unfasten his pants, but he didn't. He sat across from her, smiling slightly, while she lay exposed to him. She became self-conscious and started to straighten up, but he stopped her with a shake of his head.

"No, don't move. I want to look at you."

Suzanne sank back against the cushions her legs splayed apart, her juices leaking. What kind of man was Brian? A little perverted, sure, but she liked it. She wondered if any of the other "finalists" were giving him this kind of show. She had to assume they were—they'd be fools not to.

"Unbutton your top." It was a command.

Suzanne found herself obeying. She unfastened the top four buttons and pulled the material apart, exposing her heaving breasts. She smiled a sly little smile and let him take a good look. She fully expected him to fuck her now.

"Looks like we're here." The limo slowed to a stop.

Dammit! She mentally cursed her luck before catching herself. She'd just invite him upstairs, no problem. She began to gather herself.

"Wait."

She paused, uncertain. She felt the driver get out, the door clumped closed behind him. She could visualize him walking around the car to the rear door. She wanted to cover up, but she didn't, waiting for Brian's signal. It was so deliciously naughty and so terribly embarrassing at the same time.

The door opened and Suzanne did finally gasp and sit up, closing her legs. She felt like a slut.

"Oh, sorry," Baba said and closed the door immediately.

Brian smiled. "You were great." He nodded at her, as if giving permission for her to dress. She buttoned herself up quickly and smoothed down her dress, trying to maintain some dignity. She had just exposed herself to the damn limo driver and now she was trying to maintain dignity? What dignity?

It's okay – it's what Brian wanted. That made everything all right.

Brian rapped his knuckles on the window and Baba opened the door again, helping Suzanne from the car. She glanced at him, but he was discreet enough to keep his eyes averted. Brian got out behind her. He walked her to the door.

"W-would you like to come up?" She needed him now more than ever.

"Not tonight. But I'm looking forward to this weekend." Even as he spoke, he moved closer to her, pressing her against her door. He leaned down and kissed her gently on the lips again, a prolonged kiss, one that sent shivers through her. She could smell her scent on both their cheeks.

She lost herself in those lips, giving back as strong as she was getting, trying to convince him that he didn't want to go home just yet. Suzanne felt his hand on her thigh and didn't resist as it slipped underneath her dress and sidled up the outside to cup the soft edge of her ass. Her dress rode up and she was sure that passersby could see her, half exposed. She didn't care—and she didn't try to stop him. She was his. *Take me!*

They clung to each other for a few delicious seconds before Brian pulled away.

"Later," he said. "I want you to be ready." Then he was gone.

Suzanne felt an emptiness in her as she watched him walk away. *Shit, how much more ready could I be?*

Chapter Nineteen

Suzanne rubbed the vibrator over her clit and experienced her fourth orgasm. She groaned and writhed on the bed. Sweat soaked the sheets and the odor of her sex hung heavy in the room. Her dress lay in disarray on the floor by the bed. It had only been twenty minutes since Brian had walked her to the door.

She had practically run up the stairs after their goodnight kiss. She could still feel his fingerprints on her thighs. Now that she was inside, she was shocked by her behavior—so open, so slutty, so available. What if her neighbors had seen her? What would they think?

Suzanne had been far too horny to call Wendy as she had promised she would. Instead, she stripped down, grabbed her trusty vibrator and jumped into bed. She had only to touch the buzzing tool to her clit to bring herself to her fourth orgasm of the night. The image of Brian, looming over her, remained fresh in her mind.

She took more time with her next orgasm, letting it build, imagining Brian touching her. Her clit seemed raw and distended, yet she couldn't stop. She put down the vibrator and used her fingers, gently coating herself with her juices, protecting her swollen clit. Her mind raced ahead to this mysterious island and what might transpire there. Her fingers moved faster—her world collapsed down to the naked body of Brian and her own burning need. When she came for the fifth time that evening, she arched her back and groaned loudly, not caring if anyone heard through the thin walls of her apartment.

Damn, he made her so hot! She had never experienced lust like that before. She would have done anything for him at that moment. What's more, she trusted him completely—why, she couldn't explain.

She hoped he wouldn't betray her.

The phone startled her. Suzanne rolled over and wiped her tangled hair from her forehead, coming down from her post-orgasmic high. When she could breath normally again, she reached for it. The room reeked of her sex.

"Hello?" she croaked.

"Suzanne? Is that you? You sound funny. Did you just get back?"

"Um, yeah, pretty much." She coughed to clear her throat.

"How did it go? Did you have fun? Did you fuck him? Come on, spill it, girl!"

"I'm not sure I can begin to describe it," Suzanne said. She sat up and wondered where to begin. She told her of the attack by the two men outside the restaurant.

"Oh, my god! Are you all right? Did you call the police?"

"No. I mean, yes, I'm all right and no, we didn't call the police. We decided we'd rather go have dinner."

"Jeez! That's…wild. I'd've been a basket case."

"Well, you should've seen him. He disarmed one and scared off the other in just a couple of seconds. I didn't have time to really get scared."

"So how about the rest of the evening?"

Suzanne filled her in on the dinner and the walk along the Embarcadero, but she couldn't form the words to describe the ride home

"That's it? No fucking?"

"No fucking. Sorry."

Wendy seemed nonplussed. "Well…didn't all that make you want to jump his bones?"

"Well, yeah, it did."

"And he didn't make any moves on you?"

Suzanne knew her friend wouldn't let it go, so she invented a more plausible explanation of the events in the limo. "Well, in the limo on the way home, he did…um…" How could she describe what happened?

"Come on, spill it, girlfriend!"

"Well, he, um, made me come."

"Did he fuck you?"

"No."

"He didn't? So, it was just a hand-job? Or maybe…? Oh, you've got to tell me! I tell you all about my adventures!"

Suzanne tried to explain, as best she could, how Brian made her climax in the car and the sensation of being under his control.

"Oh my god! You just lay there, letting everything hang out while the butler opened the door."

"You mean driver."

"Whatever. God, girl, you got it bad!" Suzanne paused. "So, um, what did he think of your little surprise?"

"Oh, I'd say he liked it."

"See? But it sounds like you didn't need to give him any encouragement. I can't believe he didn't fuck you."

"I can't either. I wouldn't have stopped him, that's for sure."

"So I guess you had to resort to good ol' Daddy Duracell then, huh?"

Suzanne snorted. "What do you think?"

Wendy's laughter echoed down the phone line. "Did he say if he wanted to see you again?"

"Yes, as a matter of fact, he did. He invited me to his *private island*." She emphasized the last two words.

Wendy squealed. "That's perfect! Tell me all about it. Think you'll finally get laid?"

"I'd better!" If she didn't, she'd be catching the first boat to the mainland. "I don't know much about the island. He said it's in a lake up north and that it's very secluded."

"So, do you like this guy? I mean, really like him?"

"I'd have to say yes."

"You'd better pull out all the stops, lady. You don't want to get all coy and shy on this guy. When he makes his move, you'd better drop down and spread 'em!"

Suzanne laughed at the mental image. She needed no encouragement that was for sure. "Goodnight, Wen. I'll talk to you tomorrow."

"'Night, dear."

Chapter Twenty

November began with an Indian summer's grace, with temperatures still in the high seventies and only a light breeze to warn of the coming rainy season.

At the warehouse, they were experiencing a whisper of the Christmas rush, as orders slowly increased over the post-school-opening letdown. But Suzanne could hardly concentrate on her duties. Her mind kept flashing back to the limo ride, Brian's strong hands, the way she felt in his presence. Like a teenager again.

She couldn't eat and sleep came fitfully. Sometimes her dreams were about the two of them on this mysterious island, running naked through the trees, teasing each other. Other times, she was the damsel in distress, being protected as her fierce warrior battled demons and thugs. But the dream that eluded her, though she desperately wanted it, was about their lovemaking. Oh, she came close many times. The dreams had the same theme—Brian would be holding her, his hands possessing her and her clothes would fall away from her body. In each case, however, something would interrupt them. A phone call. The doorbell. Once it was even Wendy, who came in to tell Suzanne she knew what she had to do to land Brian.

"Wendy," she had screeched in her dream, "can't you see I'm *busy*!"

For some reason, her mind couldn't conceive of Brian's lovemaking, as if comparing it to her past lovers would be inadequate somehow.

So, she drifted through the days, waiting for Brian's call and fearing that he wouldn't.

"Maybe he chose someone else for this island getaway," she wailed to Wendy. It was Tuesday, four days after her last date with Brian. "Why doesn't he call me?"

Wendy poured her another glass of wine and sat back. "Now, Suze, he'll call. He's just a mysterious guy. Maybe he likes the woman to anticipate a little."

"Squirm is more like it!"

"He's a busy man. Maybe he was called away to solve a supply problem in Malaysia or something."

"He doesn't have a plant in Malaysia!" she cried.

"Okay, okay. Calm down. You know what I meant. Would you like me to track the guy down? I could call him at his office and tell him in no uncertain terms—"

"Don't you dare!" Suzanne looked horrified.

Wendy had to grin. "I wouldn't really do that. I'm just pulling your chain a little."

"I'm not in the mood." Suzanne crossed her arms under her breasts. "Look, Wen. You get guys all the time, so you can toss away the bad ones and hang onto the good ones…"

Wendy snorted.

"…but I don't date that much. So when I finally find a good one, I want to hang onto him."

"Too bad you didn't fuck him. That always seems to bring them back."

"He didn't want to!" Suzanne said with exasperation. "No, he wanted to, he just, um, didn't do it."

"Why not?"

"I think he was testing himself. Maybe me too, for all I know. He had me all puddled down there on the leather seat, spread open and ready for him and we got to my apartment, which kinda broke the mood." She had trouble explaining it, how she vibrated to his every touch, anticipated the lovemaking that she knew would come eventually.

"I don't think he and I would get along. If I had met a guy like this, I'd have to *insist* that he fuck me regularly."

For the first time, Suzanne could see why Brian didn't choose Wendy. She was too headstrong. Suzanne didn't know how Brian could have determined that so early in the selection process but somehow he did. Maybe it was the way she looked in the photos, as if her eyes had challenged him.

The phone rang, freezing them in place. They stared at each other like two young teens caught with a *Playgirl* magazine.

The phone rang again, galvanizing Suzanne to action. She spilled the wine as she jumped up, but didn't care. It was white anyway. She raced to the phone and caught it in the middle of the third ring.

"Hel-hello," she said breathlessly. Her eyes were as large as the bottoms of shot glasses as she stared at Wendy across the room.

"Hello, Suzanne?"

Suzanne put her hand over the phone and nodded vigorously. Then she snatched away her hand and said smoothly, "Oh, hi, Brian." Wendy put the back of her hand to her forehead in a false swoon and batted her eyelashes. Suzanne turned her back so she wouldn't laugh.

"Did I catch you at a bad time?"

"Oh, no. I was, I was just, I was just, um, getting some wine out of the fridge."

"Well, I called to see if you'd still like to spend the weekend with me."

"YES! I mean, yes, that's fine. I've thought about it and it seems fine." Suzanne realized she was close to babbling incoherently. She could feel his voice in her soul. She turned around and looked exasperatedly at Wendy.

"I had a good time with you. Both dates. I hope you did too." Brian's voice made her wet. She could feel the vibrations start anew.

"Oh, yes! I did too!" She saw Wendy make calming gestures with both hands, moving them palms down. Suzanne took a silent, slow breath. "What should I bring?"

"Just pack light. It's very informal out there. Swimsuit, shorts—that sort of thing. We'll be eating in both nights."

Suzanne found herself nodding, her mind already on the island with Brian.

"Suzanne?"

"Oh, yes! That sounds fine. Great! When should I be ready? Will Baba pick me up? How will we get there?"

Wendy rolled her eyes at her.

"Whoa! Hang on! I'll pick you up Friday at seven. I'll be coming alone in my SUV. It only takes a couple of hours to drive to Clear Lake. Will that be all right?"

"Yes, yes, that will be fine, just fine!" Suzanne bit her lip to stop her from saying "fine" again.

"All right, see you then. I'm looking forward to it."

"Okay. Me too. Bye!" She hung up. Her hand shook. The vibrations eased. She took a deep breath to calm her nerves.

"That was the most pitiful display of emotions I've ever seen," Wendy said. "Reminds me of the time the football quarterback said 'hi' to you in the hallway at Flagstone High. As I recall, you tripped over a garbage can."

Suzanne blushed. "God. I'm such an idiot! I'm sure he thinks I'm a giddy little schoolgirl."

"So what's the story?"

"He confirmed our date for his *private island* at Clear Lake," Suzanne couldn't help but emphasize the words. "This Friday. God, that doesn't give me much time to get ready!"

Wendy smiled. "All you really need is a toothbrush. I'm sure you won't be needing many clothes." She gave her an exaggerated wink.

"God, do ya think? Jeez, I hope so!" Suzanne wanted to fill in the blanks her dreams had left out. Put some action to the passion.

"He gonna have the limo pick you up?"

"No, this time, he's going to drive me himself! In his SUV."

"Ohh! Sounds like you two will finally be completely alone."

"That's right," Suzanne grinned salaciously. "Just me and the hunk. I'm gonna get laid this weekend!" She high-fived her friend.

"Hey!" Wendy said suddenly. "Can I come? I won't participate in the orgy, I'll just watch, maybe take some snapshots…"

Suzanne threw a couch pillow at her.

* * * * *

Sitting in his car a half-block away, Sam bit his lip as he listened to his ex-wife and her friend talk, holding the earpiece in place and plugging his other ear to block out the traffic noise. The voices of his ex and that honey-blonde best friend washed over him. He imagined what it might be like to have both of them alone together.

"Oh, baby, I've been waiting for you…" he said under his breath.

His hand dropped down to his groin and he rubbed his hardness there. He opened his eyes and looked around. He was alone on the darkened street. *Why not?* he thought and unzipped his pants. His cock sprang free—he wasn't wearing underwear. He grasped the turgid shaft and began rubbing it, imagining what it would be like to fuck Wendy while his ex watched. She'd be tied up, of course, forced to watch him plow his big cock into Wendy's mouth, ass and cunt. The cute blonde would be fighting him at first, then she'd start to get into it.

His hand moved up and down as he imagined the scene. His cock felt huge in his fist. His fantasies in his cell never included any of Suzanne's friends before. This was just a bonus. He pictured Wendy's face, lolling back, half afraid and half satiated as he pounded her. She'd scream with pleasure and Suzanne would close her eyes in disgust at her friend's betrayal.

Sam didn't want to come yet. He wanted to save that thrill imagining what he would do to his treacherous ex-wife. He loosened his grip, already dismissing Wendy from his mind. In his fantasy, she would be limp with exhaustion, unable to move. He'd untie Suzanne. She'd fight him, of course, and he'd have to slap her around a bit until she cooperated.

His cock throbbed as he visualized the scene. She'd be begging him, begging Wendy for help, but it would be useless. His hand moved up and down, making his balls ache for release. He'd make Suzy plead to be used. She'd know there was no way out. She never liked anal sex, that bitch, and he would fuck her in the ass while listening to her scream, her veins standing out on her neck, her eyes wide with fright and pain. He'd slap her ass again and again, making it bright red, forcing her to squeal for him, squeal you bitch—

He came suddenly, his seed spurting up onto his shirt. He smiled, listening to their voices. The release only teased him. He wiped the sperm off on his pant leg and let his imagination turn to his plans for her. *Private island, huh?* Sounded like the perfect set up. Now, what to do about it? He zipped up and thought the problem through.

He knew he had to check in with his probation officer back in San Jose on Thursday. But that wouldn't be a problem. He'd have plenty of time to prepare for the weekend.

His anger at Armstrong's thwarting of his earlier plans had mellowed. *It might work out for the best, after all,* he thought. His burning desire to get even with Suzanne was now tempered with greed. Armstrong was rich, so he definitely wanted to get himself a piece of that. Was there a way to do both, and leave no trace? He didn't want to involve others, like those two nitwits Jarvis and Mack so he'd have to do it himself.

Slowly, an idea began to coalesce in his mind. It needed a little preparation, a few extra items. He stared at the radio, nodding. He flicked it off and prepared to drive home, a grin spreading over his face.

"Suzanne, you are in for one hell of a surprise."

Chapter Twenty-One

"You know, there is something that occurred to me," Wendy said, taking a sip of her martini. It was the following afternoon. Suzanne had met her friend at their favorite bar—a fern place around the corner from Market Street named "The Pump Station". It had been a firehouse back in the twenties that had been sold many times since then. It had become a good place to meet horny men, probably because of the name. Now, with the late afternoon sun slanting through the narrow windows, the place was only half full.

Suzanne stopped, a glass of wine halfway to her lips. "What?" She didn't like the sound of Wendy's voice.

"This business about Brian not fucking you when he had the chance—hell, when you practically threw yourself at him."

"What about it?"

"It makes me wonder if he's got something to hide."

Suzanne was becoming exasperated. "Yeah? Like what? What are you getting at?"

"Well, I don't want to worry you..."

"Wendy!"

"Okay, okay." She waved her hand. "It's probably nothing. It seemed odd, that a healthy man like that wouldn't go for it. What is it they say about men and making love? 'They don't need a reason, they only need a place.' So I thought, maybe...you know..."

Suzanne had no idea what Wendy was trying to say. Her blank expression must've conveyed her confusion, for Wendy hurried on…

"You know, maybe his, um, equipment, um…"

Suzanne sat back in her chair. "You think he's impotent!"

A couple at a nearby table glanced over sharply. Suzanne's face grew hot. She dropped her voice to a whisper.

"You're saying you think Brian can't get it up?"

"That, or maybe, you know…" She held up her little finger and wiggled it.

"Oh, my God!" Such thoughts had never occurred to her. Now what Wendy had said made a certain amount of sense. Brian enjoyed control, but didn't take advantage of her. He liked her to be exposed, but didn't stare. He didn't encourage her to touch him, so she had no idea if he had gotten an erection—or what size it might've been.

"You think that his…" Suzanne couldn't say the word.

Wendy shrugged. "It's a possibility. Jim and the twins could be non-op." She giggled. "Or midgets."

"That's not funny!"

"Sorry. You're right. I'm sure I'm just letting my imagination run free. Maybe it's his little fetish—you know, looking but not touching. I've seen far stranger ones."

Suzanne nodded, trying to convince herself that there was nothing more to it. Still, the doubts Wendy planted remained.

"What if it's true? That he can't, you know, perform. What should I do?"

"Do? What can you do? Cry, I guess." Wendy leaned closer. "But if it were me, I'd be sure and pack my vibrator."

*****

Suzanne, fresh from her shower and still dressed in her red rayon robe, packed carefully for the trip. She included shorts, T-shirts, a skirt and blouse, a simple black dress in case he changed his mind and decided to take her out to dinner, a few pairs of shoes, including sneakers, and several different styles of bras and panties. She wanted to be able to anticipate Brian's moods. She rummaged through her underwear drawer, selecting some of her sexiest panties and bras, then whittled down the list until she had three of each—slutty, sluttier and sluttiest. Wendy would be so proud of her.

Of course, she'd need a bathing suit. She selected a one-piece that had been flattering the last time she'd worn it. She wished she had time to go buy a bikini, but maybe that was being too bold.

Next, she added her bathroom items, including her most valuable possession, her hairdryer. *He'd better have electricity out there,* she thought, *or I'm going to look like Carrot Top.*

Finally, she tossed in two three-packs of condoms, hoping that she would be able to use them. She was past the point of thinking Brian's actions were noble or gentlemanly. Now she just wanted to be taken, hard and fast.

What if it's true! her mind wailed. *What if he's a lousy lover?*

That'd be just my luck, her dark thoughts pouted. *Find a great guy and it turns out he's limp as a noodle.*

Come on! Her positive side responded. *He's probably a great lover. Besides, there's a lot more to a man than that! Think about how kind and strong, and special he is! Hell, you can fake the rest.*

She tried to agree, but she could hear the dark side of her personality laughing rudely at her. *Better do as Wendy says and pack Daddy Duracell! Bring extra batteries!*

Suzanne shrugged off her robe and folded it carefully on top. This was her travel robe, but she really considered it her seducing robe. She doubted Brian could resist the hot color, the silk-like feel of it, the way it slipped from her body…

She shook her head. She looked down at herself, making sure her little lightning bolt stood out well against her white skin. She almost had shaved it off completely, since Brian hadn't paid much attention to it. *I mean, what the hell?* she thought. But at the last minute, she decided to shave around it one more time. It had seemed like a lark at the time, but now she felt slightly ridiculous. *I don't know how I let Wendy talk me into this!*

Of course, she knew. Suzanne long ago had realized that Wendy was the "alpha female" in their relationship. Suzanne didn't mind, in fact, she liked letting Wendy make the decisions about what they would do or where they would go. Wendy was action, Suzanne reaction.

That's not to say that Suzanne did everything Wendy did. Certainly, she was more circumspect about her relationships with men. Yet, she realized that Brian was attracted to her because she was a follower. She had bested other women in this strange little contest because she had the qualities he liked.

For the first time, Suzanne was beginning to understand what Brian had meant when he advertised for a "kept woman". He could have just as easily called for an "old-fashioned woman".

Shaking herself out of her reverie, she glanced at the clock. Six-twenty! He'd be here in forty minutes! "Aakk! You're still naked, you dummy!" she scolded herself and ran to the bathroom to get ready.

With five minutes to spare, Suzanne plopped her small suitcase next to the couch and sat down, nervous and exhilarated. She wore new blue jeans, a yellow T-shirt and tennis shoes. She hoped he wouldn't show up in a dinner jacket. Mentally, she went over the items in her overnight bag, making sure she hadn't forgotten anything. Like many women, she had a tendency to over-pack and the bulging bag attested to it.

The buzzer rang, startling her, though she had expected it. Shaking, she got up slowly from the couch and walked unsteadily to the panel by the door.

"Yes?" she said into the intercom.

"It's me." Suzanne recognized Brian's voice immediately. She buzzed him in. She could feel her loins contract and expand. *He's not even in the room yet and I'm already horny!*

In a few minutes, she heard his knock at her door. She spread her fingers and shook her hands hard like pompoms to quell her nerves before she opened the door. "Hi, Brian. Come on it. I'm just about ready."

He smiled when he saw her and stepped inside. Brian was dressed in tan slacks, a green polo shirt and casual loafers. He looked good enough to eat.

He leaned down to kiss her, letting one hand rest possessively on her ass. He squeezed it as he kissed her.

Had he taken her to the bedroom right then, she would've gone along willingly.

Brian pulled back, eyeing her speculatively. His eyes slid over to her suitcase. "Packing for a week?" he teased.

"I know. I tend to overdo it. I just didn't know what to expect…uh, weather-wise," she added hastily. She stepped back. "Did I dress appropriately? I thought it might get cool later, so…" Her voice trailed off.

Brian studied her for a moment. "Well, you look very nice. But for this weekend, I had something else in mind. I mean, if you're willing…"

Suzanne bit her lip. She had tried to anticipate what he'd like. How had she gone wrong?

"What-what kind of outfit would you prefer?"

He gave her a half-grin. "Oh, maybe a skirt? And a blouse that buttons down the front?"

Suzanne nearly slapped her forehead. She should've known. He wanted to start right off, making her pliable, keeping her horny during the ride north. She grabbed her suitcase, saying, "I'll be right back," and disappeared into the room.

Suzanne opened the case and picked out a simple blue skirt and white blouse. She quickly stripped off her clothes and started to put the jeans inside her suitcase, then stopped. She tossed them on the bed, along with the T-shirt. *He won't want those,* she told herself. In fact, looking through her outfits, she realized there were a few other items she could get rid off—the pantyhose, the slacks, the sweatshirt… In seconds, she had reduced the contents of the bag by one-third.

She stopped for a moment, struck by a twinge of Women's Lib guilt. *Am I being disloyal to women everywhere by catering to this man?* It was a legitimate question. *Then again,* she thought, *he's pretty terrific. And I like the way he makes me feel. So there.*

Her conscience assuaged, she started to slip into her new outfit but paused again. *I know what he'd really like,* the naughty side of her spoke up. Nodding to herself, she stood there a moment longer, contemplating. She always had been a good girl, but right now, she wanted to be bad, very bad. Wendy bad. Before she could change her mind, she stripped off her bra and slipped off her panties, and donned the blouse and skirt.

She felt like a different woman, open and free, and unbelievably wicked. The air teased her naked slit. She adjusted her skirt, noting that it fell to just above her knees, so at least she didn't feel too slutty. But her breasts underneath her blouse jiggled obscenely, she thought. She experimented in front of the mirror, moving around while she watched the nipples gyrate against the cotton material. Fortunately, the blouse wasn't entirely see-through. Still, Brian—and anybody else, for that matter—could instantly tell she wasn't wearing a bra.

Am I going too far? She stared at her reflection in the mirror. She realized, for perhaps the first time in her life that she had been the good girl for too long. Yes, this was what Brian wanted, but this was what she wanted as well.

She fluffed her hair, then closed her suitcase and returned to the living room.

"Here, let me take that," he said automatically then stopped, as if he'd been poleaxed. He stared at her breasts unabashedly. A slow smile formed on his face and broadened into a toothy grin.

"You look…wonderful," he said.

Suzanne blushed. She felt pleased.

"What about..." Brian wiggled his fingers at her skirt.

"That's for me to know and you to find out," she retorted, smiling. She wondered if he could smell the slight scent of her sex. Unconsciously, she moved her legs apart to allow more air to circulate.

God, she thought. *I'm like those animals on National Geographic. When the females want to mate, they let the males know in no uncertain terms. Could I be any more obvious?*

He reached for her suddenly, causing her to gasp as he drew her into his arms. His mouth was on hers. Like before, his kiss was gentle but insistent. She responded, wishing he'd just jump her now and get it over with. Instead, his hand dropped down to lift her skirt so his could slide his hand up along the outside of her leg to her naked ass. She sighed, knowing that he was simply going to tease her.

How long will this go on before I explode?

He broke away, that wry grin on his face. "Naughty girl," he said, patting her smooth flesh before letting his hand slip away. "Come on, let's hit the road."

He carried her suitcase out to the car, a new, black SUV with tinted windows and all the extras. He put her gear in next to his small overnight bag and opened the passenger door for her. He gave her a half bow and held up one hand to give her support as she climbed up into the cab.

Suzanne luxuriated in the plush interior, adjusting her skirt to cover her nudity. Again, she felt the passions stirring within her. Here she was, about to embark on an adventure with a handsome, charismatic, rich man, but more important than all those qualities—and they *were* important—was her trust in Brian. He made her feel safe, like she could allow her true self to emerge.

The question remained, who was her true self? She'd been quietly repressing herself for so long, she hardly knew what she wanted anymore. She felt like someone who had been on a diet for the last twenty years, suddenly seated in front of an enormous meal and told to help herself.

Could I help myself to Brian and all he offers? Or is it all too good to be true?

Brian steered the car away from her apartment building and headed for the northbound onramp of Highway 101. Once on the freeway, Suzanne put her questions away and just enjoyed the ride.

They chatted for a while about innocuous things, their conversation flowing like they were old friends. The sun was low on the horizon, beginning to slide into the sea as they headed north, washing the sky with colors. To Suzanne, it was as if they were entering a new world, one far away from the day-to-day drudgery her life had become. She had been a caterpillar and now she wanted to see how the butterflies lived.

"Hike your skirt up a little," Brian's voice cut through her daydreaming.

"Huh?"

"I said, hike up your skirt a little. I'd like to see a little more skin."

Automatically, she moved to obey. "I wouldn't want you to have a wreck," she teased. She brought her skirt right up to the top of her thighs, hinting at the treasure above.

Brian nodded. "That's good. Just enough to tease me. I'll try to keep us on the road."

Suzanne let her eyes slide over his pants, but couldn't see if his body was responding to her. She decided to up the ante. She reached up and unbuttoned the top two buttons, allowing more of her cleavage to show.

She leaned forward and turned slightly toward him, showing off. She had never felt so wicked!

Brian grinned at her and winked. She glanced down at his slacks and thought she saw a stirring there. It gave her hope that Wendy had been wrong.

*****

Sam followed well behind, listening to a country-western station and smoking cigarettes. Occasionally, he glanced down at the electronic device on the passenger seat that beeped regularly, indicating Armstrong's position.

It had been so easy to sneak up and attach the tracker to his bumper while Brian had been inside. Now he just had to drive along and follow the signal.

Just like 007, he thought. *License to kill.*

A goofy grin lit up his face at his own dark humor. He couldn't wait to see Suzanne's expression when he showed up on Armstrong's island. God, that would be rich!

In the trunk, he carried everything he'd need to make this weekend special.

Chapter Twenty-Two

Suzanne, tired from a long week at work, dozed off as the car glided smoothly into the fading light. She felt completely relaxed, though she knew passing truckers could see her skirt hiked up and her half-opened blouse. It didn't matter.

Did it?

She awoke as the car bumped down a gravel road. The headlights, on full beam, showed them to be in the middle of a forest.

"Where are we?" She sat up groggily and automatically adjusted her skirt down.

"Almost there. You were conked out for most of the time."

"Sorry. I hope you weren't too bored."

"No, no. It's not a long trip." Brian turned the wheel and the SUV bounced down a narrow trail, ending at an old wooden dock by the quiet lake.

"It's nice," she said, though there wasn't much to see. The headlights reflected off the surface but she couldn't see the island.

"How far out is it?"

"Not too far. Just a half-mile or so."

They got out. Brian brought the suitcases around and led her to the dock. A small fiberglass boat with an outboard motor lay tied up along the far side. He placed the suitcases in the middle and helped Suzanne down into the padded seat up front. He sat in back.

"Let's hope this starts."

Suzanne smiled. "It could be a short trip." *If it doesn't start, I'm taking him to the nearest motel. You owe me a powerful fucking, mister!*

He cranked the outboard. It sputtered and died. He pulled hard again and the motor caught. It roared for a moment and he adjusted it to a lower pitch. He reached up and untied the line.

The roar of the motor prevented much conversation. She sat in the bow of the boat and looked into the darkness, feeling the cool mist from the spray wafting over her.

The ride didn't last long. Within a few minutes, a shape loomed up in the darkness. Brian steered the boat alongside it. Suzanne could see it was a narrow island, full of scrubby trees and bushes that widened as they sped along.

"It's called Rattlesnake Island," Brian shouted over the motor. "But don't worry, there are no snakes. It's named for its shape."

Suzanne nodded and watched the island undulate as they sped alongside. It did have a snake-like look to it, twisting in and out, creating coves and inlets along the side. They came to the far end, where it ended in a large knob, like the head of a snake. As he circled around, she saw through the gloom a white, two-story house with a wraparound porch at the second level. It remained partially hidden by the trees and was illuminated by a single light near the well-kept dock. Brian slowed and steered the boat to it.

He shut the motor off and they drifted alongside. He grabbed a line and jumped onto the dock, fastening it tight to a pier. He went to the bow and asked Suzanne to toss him the second line and he snugged it tight as well.

Brian helped her off. She watched as he grabbed the suitcases then with a toss of his head, led her to the house. Suzanne studied it as they approached. It looked quite new.

"It's beautiful," she said.

"This was built about five years ago, so it's got all the modern conveniences." He unlocked the door and ushered her inside. He flicked a switch by the door and one small light barely pierced the gloom.

"This light and the dock light are on solar-powered batteries that constantly recharge. Hang on while I get out some lanterns. Then I'll go fire up the main generator."

He went off into the darkness, returning a minute later with a softly glowing lantern. The flame cast eerie shadows along the walls. A darkened one was in his other hand. He put the light down on a table and lit the second one.

"There, that's better."

Suzanne looked around. The living room was paneled in cherry, giving the cabin a rustic feel. A soot-blackened fireplace stood at one end. The furniture looked comfortable and inviting.

"This is a great getaway," she said.

"Come on," he said, picking up a lantern. "I'll show you the kitchen."

He gave her a quick tour. The kitchen was spotless, with granite counters and an island. To Suzanne, it appeared like something out of *Country Living*.

She heard a humming and turned, surprised to hear the refrigerator operating. She asked him about it.

"Oh, that's gas-powered. Keeps it cold all the time. Otherwise, well, you know how old refrigerators smell."

She opened it and observed enough food for several days. "Well, we won't be going hungry."

"Yeah. I wasn't sure what we needed so I had the caretaker put in a little of everything. Let me get the generator going, then I'll show you the upstairs."

He went out the back door with one of the lanterns and in a few minutes, Suzanne could hear the low rumble of the main generator. Lights began coming on throughout the house.

Brian returned, grinning and blew out the lantern. "That went well. I made sure the caretaker checked it before he left. Wouldn't want to get stranded out here with no juice."

Suzanne thought the lantern light was rather romantic, but she didn't say anything. She half-expected him to reveal a big-screen TV behind a panel and settle down in the couch with a beer. Of course, that's what a typical man would do. She didn't really think Brian was typical.

"Come on," he said, grabbing her suitcase. "I'll show you your room."

My room?

"Hey," she said suddenly. He turned. "You're going to make me sleep in my own room?"

"Probably not. I'm just going slow. I like to heighten the experience. It's like the difference between a woman in a sexy negligee versus one naked. The former hints at the delights to come, while the latter lays it all out, removing all the secrets."

"Well, considering what's gone on between us, we don't have many secrets left, do we?"

Brian's grin lit up. "No, I guess we don't."

He didn't know how wrong he was.

Chapter Twenty-Three

Sam parked a quarter-mile from the shore and turned off the insistent beeping of the tracker. He didn't dare get too close in case they were still near the car. He stepped out and walked as quietly as he could down the crude road until he spotted the dark shape of the SUV in the moonlight.

He paused, listening. He didn't want to ruin everything before he started. Reaching behind him, he eased the Glock out of his waistband at the small of his back and held it down along his thigh.

Sam crept closer, his ears turned to every sound. He crept up to the driver's side and saw nothing. A peek inside told him they were gone.

He walked to the dock and cursed when he noticed there were no boats for him to steal. He turned and began to walk along the shore. He'd find one somewhere.

The question was, which way did they go? He couldn't see any islands in the darkness. The idea of him out boating around in the dark didn't appeal to him. He knew Suzanne and this Armstrong asshole were going to be there for the weekend so what was the rush?

He could rent a comfy little motel room and come back in the morning, early. *Banks are open until noon, aren't they?* He nodded, as if winning the argument with himself. He stopped and retraced his steps, heading back to his car.

He had plenty of time. Once he had the money, he might enjoy tormenting Suzanne for a while before putting the final part of his plan into place.

*****

Suzanne tried to be coy, but when Brian approached her, his arms wide, she nearly leapt into his grasp. The feel of his muscled chest, the manly smell of him, the taste of his lips on hers made her lightheaded.

He held her delicately when she wanted to be crushed. He kissed her softly when she wanted a demanding French kiss. She couldn't explain it. It just was. But that was all right. He controlled the pace of their lovemaking. She knew he liked to lead the way.

She wrestled with her emotions, trying to match her needs with his actions. When he slipped a hand underneath her skirt, she mentally gave herself a high-five. *There ya go!* His hand seemed hot against her naked flesh. It sent goose bumps up and down her body.

He kissed her mouth, her neck, her ear. His hand brushed the V of her legs and she shuddered anew. His fingers came away wet.

"Let's go upstairs," he whispered.

She could only nod.

He took her hand and led her up the steps. The master bedroom was decorated in a masculine country style, with stressed pine on the walls and a simple, Quaker-style queen-sized bed.

Brian led her to it and sat down, holding her slender body between his legs. "I've really been looking forward to this," he murmured, as his hands touched her thighs under her skirt.

You and me both, buster! she thought, but said nothing. She could feel tears come to her eyes—tears of joy and anticipation.

He brought her closer letting his hands roam more possessively over her body. She wanted to strip right now and jump naked into the bed, let Brian crush her with his body.

He reached up and brought her head down so he could kiss her again. She pressed hard against him, letting her body telegraph her urgency.

Brian unzipped her skirt and let it fall away. He pulled away for a moment and grinned at her lightning bolt. "This is so cool," he said.

"You like?"

"Oh, yeah. My little electric girl." He spun her around and let her fall onto the bed. In seconds, he'd dived down to her wet slit, lapping greedily.

Suzanne swooned and spread her legs for him. Her blouse suddenly seemed too hot for her so she unbuttoned it and let the sides fall apart, exposing her breasts.

Brian gently licked at her, causing her clitoris to swell. In minutes, she could feel a powerful orgasm developing. She closed her eyes and lost herself in it.

"Oh, god! Oh my god!" she cried as the sensation peaked within her. All other thoughts disappeared from her mind. She had become a sexual beast, good only for orgasms.

She watched as Brian removed his clothes. She had been waiting for this moment forever. He peeled off his shirt, revealing a well-toned stomach and chest. It was better than she had hoped. She held her breath as he unzipped his pants. She heard a building crescendo in her head as his cock sprang free. It was perfect. Not too big, not too small. The music in her head swelled along with his cock.

He caught her looking at his groin. "You like?"

"Oh yes. It's perfect." She reached out to gently grasp it in her right hand. It pulsed in her fingers.

Brian moved up over her. He stopped to taste her nipples. Every touch electrified her, every thought was about his cock and how it would feel inside her. Her nipples ached. She could feel it in her clit too.

He leaned in close to her ear. "I'm going to fuck you now," he whispered.

Yes! Yes! her id shouted. Her ego was more practical. "Put on a condom," she said.

Brian paused to slip one on over his turgid cock. She opened herself even more, fearing nothing now. She had been waiting for this for a long time. All her doubts, all Wendy's concerns, evaporated. She was a vessel, waiting to be filled.

Brian's cock slipped into her easily, as if was meant to be there. Her pussy grasped at him, pulled him in. Her mouth fell open the sensations were almost too much to bear.

"Yesss," she breathed. She could tell the orgasm she had attained when he tongued her was only a precursor for what was to come, like a tiny shock before the big earthquake.

"You are mine, all mine," Brian whispered. "I love the way you make me feel."

Suzanne couldn't speak. Her emotions—in fact her entire being—was focused somewhere below her ovaries. She felt him stroke into her then pull back. Each movement sent shivers up and down her arms, back and chest. Her nipples were painfully erect.

"God," she whispered. "Oh god, fuck me."

Brian obliged. He began moving faster now, his cock stroking in and out, each time sliding along her clit. Suzanne climbed up the ladder toward her orgasm. She couldn't believe how it built up and up and up. Her vibrator never made her feel this way! She rode with him, delighting at how in tune their bodies seemed to be. They were a natural fit together.

Brian tensed suddenly and thrust hard against her, emptying his seed. She felt his cock throb within her. He cried out, an incoherent sound. This final push against her clit caused her to erupt in a shattering orgasm. She screamed, she cried, she held him close. He gripped her tightly as his cock throbbed within her. She wrapped her legs around him, not wanting to let him go.

For several long minutes, they clung to each other before finally falling apart, exhausted. Sweat coated both their bodies.

"Jesus!" she gasped, trying to fill her lungs with air. "Jesus."

"That was amazing," Brian agreed. "I've never felt like that before. Never."

"We might be dangerous together," she managed. "Like we could explode, take out the entire island."

"Yeah, that's it. We should be placed in individual bunkers, far apart. Whenever a foreign power messed with us, they could threatened to parachute us into their country, naked."

Suzanne laughed. "Yeah. We could be Uncle Sam's secret weapon. The Sex Bomb."

"Rated fifty megatons." He leaned over and kissed her. "I'll bet you're one of those women who like to cuddle after sex."

"I hope you aren't one of those men who instantly fall asleep!"

"No." He shook his head. "I'm not going to leave you alone. But you did take the strength right out of me. This is why men fall asleep, you know. It's a sign that their women have fucked them to within an inch of their lives."

Brian hugged her and nestled his head up against her shoulder. He kissed the hollow of her neck and smelled the wonderful womanness of her. Suzanne felt a great sense of contentment. For a long time, they just lay there, wordless, satisfied.

Finally, he got up and went to the bathroom. She watched him walk away, his buns flexing. It made it her hot all over again and she shook her head. *Not now, you slut!* She smiled at her own wantonness.

Brian came out, his limp cock hanging between his legs. "I'm going to make a cup of coffee—want some?"

Suzanne smiled. She had a man who not only fucked her brains out but made coffee afterwards. "Yes. That sounds nice."

"How do you like your coffee?"

"Black is fine—if it's fresh ground. If not, maybe a little milk in it."

"It's fresh." He padded away.

Suddenly, Suzanne felt lonely. The heat of the moment had evaporated and her doubts began to creep in. Shaking her head, she rose and started to put on her robe, then decided against it. Naked, she tiptoed down the stairs. Her fluids leaked out of her and down her thighs. She didn't care.

She stood on the last step, listening to him move around in the kitchen. She didn't want to spy on him, yet she didn't want him to think she was so needy she couldn't stand to be away from him, even if just for a minute.

Suzanne shook her head. She was just being silly. She stepped down onto the wooden floor then followed him into the kitchen. Brian was bent over the coffeemaker, carefully measuring scoops from a bag. The coffee smelled wonderful.

"What kind is it?"

Brian turned. "Well, hello there, naked girl. It's Kenyan. Do you mind if it's a little strong?"

God, she thought, *I'd like it anyway you want to make it.* "Strong is fine. It's good."

"Good." He turned back, and Suzanne eyed his perfect ass again. She came closer and touched it. He wiggled it into her hand. "Did any of your other girls tell you what a nice butt you have?"

Dammit! she immediately thought. *Why'dya have to bring up the other women!*

But Brian didn't seem to mind. "Oh, all the time." She could tell he was teasing.

"Oh? They've all seen it, have they?" She pretended to be jealous.

"Didn't you get the memo? Everyone had to put out on the first date or be eliminated."

"That's funny," she said, putting her arms around him from behind. "We didn't make love on the first date."

"Yes, and you were eliminated. Didn't you know? This is just the consolation date. You see, I'm not really the CEO of the company. I'm the janitor."

She laughed and hugged him. She liked his quick wit. Suzanne reached down and touched his dick, which swelled in her hand. "Hey, for a janitor, you've sure got the right equipment for the job."

"Careful—you might get hosed!"

He turned and tickled her. The coffee perked as they giggled and grasped at each other. Suzanne had never felt such powerful emotions as this before.

Could this be love?

Or am I just in lust?

"Coffee's ready," he said, when the tale-tell bubbling of the machine finally ended. He poured them each a cup.

"Ahh," he said, taking a sip. "Nothing like a good cup of coffee after sex. I think it's the modern-day equivalent of a cigarette."

"Yes, that's true. Everyone used to smoke after sex. Drinking coffee is probably a lot healthier."

"Unless you spill it on yourself," he teased, stroking a naked breast. She giggled and pulled away from the tickling, her coffee cup steady in one hand.

"I'll be careful. You sure wouldn't want it to drip onto certain parts of yours either!" She eyed his cock.

"Yikes. That would ruin a perfectly good weekend, wouldn't it? I'd hate to have to explain that in the emergency room."

They drank for a few minutes, lost in thought, enjoying the quiet, broken only by the lap of gentle waves outside. Finally Brian spoke. "Suzanne."

"Yes?" She turned to him, gazing into his eyes, feeling more in love by the minute.

"No one else has visited this island. And I don't think anyone else will."

She let a slow smile spread across her face. "I'm glad to hear you say that, Mr. Armstrong."

Chapter Twenty-Four

Suzanne loved how the light streamed through the slats of the windows, dappling the countertops. Then again, she loved just about everything this morning. After such a powerful, emotional session of lovemaking last night, they repeated the performance again at dawn, like a couple of horny school kids.

She poured Brian some coffee and sat down from him across the small kitchen table. Both were still tousled with sleep and sex. Each wore robes, with nothing underneath, feeling very comfortable with each other. Suzanne's body felt electric. It hummed with satisfaction and desire. She hoped Brian felt the same way.

Brian took a sip from the china cup. "Thanks," he said. "It was great." Suzanne thought he meant more than the coffee.

She smiled. "Yeah." A dreamy look came to her face.

"So I guess what they say is true."

"What's that?"

"Lightning does strike twice."

She nearly choked on her coffee.

"I think there was some thunder too," he added.

For a moment, Suzanne became embarrassed, recalling her vocal responses to Brian's lovemaking. "I've never thought of myself as a screamer before," she said slyly.

"This is the perfect place for that. No one around for miles."

"It is beautiful here." To Suzanne, Motel 6 would have been beautiful if Brian was there.

"After breakfast, we can go for a walk. There are paths that lead all through the forest, such as it is."

"Looks to be a warm day. Should be perfect."

"You know, the best way to explore is, um…" Suddenly, he seemed embarrassed.

"What?"

"Naked," he said, grinning.

"You want to walk around the island naked? What about mosquitoes?"

"They don't come out here. Too far from shore, I guess. Besides, mosquitoes hate mornings."

"Well, I guess it might be okay…" She paused. "After last night and this morning, I'm probably safe from being attacked, hmmm?"

"Oh, I don't know about that." He winked.

"How can you? I mean…" Suzanne couldn't imagine he could make love again.

"Well, you're probably right about that—you wore me out pretty good there. But I still want to." He came to her and hugged her to him. "I wonder why that is."

Suzanne felt good in his arms. "I don't know—I guess I'm just so gosh-darned attractive, huh?"

"Yeah. That's it. And modest too."

She laughed. "Well, if cuddling is good enough for you, it's great for me. You probably knew that about women, didn't you?"

"What? That they're great cuddlers? Yeah, I knew. Come on." He took her by the hand and led her down the hallway to the bedroom. He stripped off her robe and pulled back the covers.

"You know, it's funny," she said, slipping under the covers.

"Yeah? What's that?"

"When I packed, I made sure to include my vibrator, in case you decided not to make love to me. I was so pent-up, I don't think I could've gone all weekend without getting laid, even if it was by a poor substitute to a real man."

"Did you think I wouldn't?"

"Well, you've been more than a gentleman, that's for sure. I was beginning to wonder if I just wasn't attractive to you."

He laughed. "That's why men won't ever understand women. We think you're all 'good girls' who don't want to be rushed but in reality, you're naughty little sluts who just want to get fucked."

The strong language only excited Suzanne more. She watched as he opened his robe. His cock stirred, as if the "Little Men" were in there mightily throwing switches and opening valves to no avail.

Brian noticed her gaze and looked down at his soft cock. "Hang on," he said and turned toward the suitcases. He began rummaging through Suzanne's. "Ah hah!" He held up her vibrator in victory.

Suzanne blushed. "Hey, I wasn't—"

He held up his free hand. "Never fear. I'm not insulted. It's only a temporary solution, until Mr. Big here wakes up from his little nap." Suzanne giggled.

He jumped on the bed, vibrator held high, causing her to squeal and pretend to try to get away. "No! Not that! Please don't throw me in that briar patch!"

"Methinks the lady protests too much." He flicked on the switch. The vibrator hummed to life. Suzanne, like Pavlov's dogs, instantly found herself wet. Brian brought it down between her legs and pressed it to her pussy. She gasped and spread her legs for him. He rotated the tip around in her juices, making sure it was coated before he began to ease it into her.

To Suzanne, it was beyond intimate. She never expected Brian to be so free and natural about their lovemaking. It was as if he was reading her mind as they went, knowing just what aroused her the most. He was a nasty lover and a perfect gentleman, all wrapped into one. An ideal man.

When the buzzing toy touched her, she shivered in anticipation. She knew she could come again, despite being well satiated by this amazing man. She knew she could do anything with him without embarrassment. She abandoned herself to her feelings and allowed the first of several orgasms to rock through her.

After forty minutes, Suzanne begged Brian to stop. She couldn't take any more. "Please, I'm limp, I'm exhausted. I need to rest my sore little pussy."

He grinned and pulled away, tossing the vibrator onto the other side of the bed. "Looks like my job is done."

She reached out to touch his semi-erect cock. "But what about you?"

"Don't worry. I'll get mine. Later. But I promised you a tour of my island. Come one, let's shower up and go."

Afterward, Brian and Suzanne returned to the kitchen, where they shared another cup of coffee. "You hungry?" he asked.

"Starving. And I'm not normally a breakfast person. I wonder what's gotten into me?"

Brian just winked at her and turned toward the refrigerator. "You want some eggs?"

"Perfect. And toast?"

"Great. You do the toast, I'll scramble some eggs."

They bustled about in the small kitchen, sidestepping each other adroitly, as if they were already used to each other's presence. They felt comfortable together.

Brian and Suzanne stepped out into the brilliant warm morning after a leisurely breakfast of eggs, toast and jam. There wasn't a soul to be seen. She felt they were alone in the world. The last couple on Earth.

"Well?" Brian said. "Are you game?"

Suzanne remembered his challenge. She untied the sash of her robe and let it puddle to her feet, exposing herself to the world, which consisted of just one man. "I am if you are, buster."

He followed suit and they laughed at their own nervousness. "Bet you can't catch me," she shouted and took off down the path leading into the woods. With a shout, Brian followed.

* * * * *

The sun had been up barely an hour when Sam cut the engine and drifted toward the island. He hoped this was the right one. It was the only one he could see from shore when he had arrived shortly after dawn.

He had no idea where they might be—he assumed there was a cabin on the island somewhere. But he didn't want to stumble on them accidentally so he chose to beach the boat in one of the little coves and walk in.

Sam used an oar to push the boat up on the tiny beach. He jumped out, ignoring the water sloshing over his shoes and used a mooring line to tie the boat off to a scrawny tree. With luck, he'd have the boat back on shore before it was missed. That was part of his plan—to seem like he had never been here at all.

He checked his Glock, making sure the safety was on. He liked the feel of it in his hand. He tucked it into his pocket, and pulled the black gym bag from the boat and hooked it over his shoulder. He entered the scrub forest.

Within five minutes, Sam found a path. Instinct told him to go right.

* * * * *

Suzanne ran along the path, enjoying the sensation of total freedom. *This is how Adam and Eve must've felt,* she thought. Years of being embarrassed to be naked dissipated. For the first time, she could understand what drove nudists to shun clothes.

She heard the pounding of feet behind her. She dodged left, down a narrower path and ran right down to the edge of a small cove. Trapped! She turned to see Brian grinning at her from the path. His hard-on half swelled.

"Oh, my, this morning air must agree with you." She pointed.

He looked down. "Um, yes. But I think it's you who agrees with me."

"So, you've caught me. You can't possibly want to ravish me again!" She hoped, of course, that he would. She had a lot of sex to catch up on. Idly, she wondered what she would be telling Wendy about this weekend.

"I think you have me at a disadvantage. The spirit is willing but the flesh is weak." He reached down and lifted his semi-erect cock gently. "The poor little guy is still tuckered out."

"Aww. Let me kiss it and make it better." She came to him and knelt into the sandy path before him. Suzanne reached out and caressed his member, getting her first close-up look at it. Even semi-hard, it was magnificent. Circumcised, bulbous and veiny, his cock could be a model for dildos everywhere. She could imagine making a mold of this one herself.

She let her fingers explore the ball-sack below. Gently, she felt the outlines of his testes, the size of small eggs. Her hand moved up to his cock. She was fascinated by it. To think that it had thrust into her hot wet core twice in the last twelve hours! And there was more to come, she was sure.

Opening her mouth, she let her tongue lick the tip. Brian shivered. "Oh, baby. You'd better be careful. You might start something you're not prepared to finish."

Suzanne could feel his cock swell in her hand already. "I sense a rallying of the troops," she breathed before taking the bulbous head into her mouth. She caressed it with her lips and tongue, delighted to find it growing further. She could feel her own wetness spreading along her slit. She reached down with one hand, completely unabashed, and began to coax her tender clit from its sheath.

She pulled back just enough to speak. "I'm a bit sore myself. We should probably stop." When Brian didn't say anything, Suzanne decided that she didn't want to stop, either. She took the head of his cock back into her mouth and licked the sweet nectar from its tip.

That brought a reaction from Brian. "Ohhh," he said. "I think the captor has become the captive."

Suzanne smiled inwardly and took more of him into her mouth. Her tongue flicked at the underside of his cock. He was almost fully erect now. She imagined his cock like an elaborate machine—"Little men" running around, opening valves and shouting orders, trying to get the huge cock erect yet again. "We can't, Captain, we don'na have the reserves!" the engineer would plead, only to be countermanded by the brain: "I've got to have more power, Scotty! Our reputation is at stake!"

Suzanne, who had learned how to deep-throat with the best of the sorority sisters in college, opened her throat to accept Brian's cock, grabbing his thighs to pull herself against him. Back and forth she moved her mouth, feeling his pleasure building.

She loved giving this man pleasure, feeling him helpless in her grasp, enjoying her technique. She sucked him harder now, and could tell he was fully erect by the way his cock fit into her mouth.

Suddenly, he grabbed the back of her head and gave an inarticulate cry. Suzanne felt his cock pump powerfully, sending warm seed into her throat. She pulled back and swallowed it quickly, relishing the taste of him, happy to have been able to coax another orgasm from his tired body.

She let his limp cock fall from her mouth. She looked up into Brian's eyes. "See what happens when you catch the girl you're chasing?"

Brian gasped. "That's it! I'll never make love again! I'm all worn out." He pulled her to her feet and hugged her fiercely. "God, woman, you're incredible. And insatiable."

Suzanne felt just right in his arms. So safe and loved. She had doubted it would've ever happened. Now, thanks to Wendy, she was here in this wonderful man's arms, feeling loved like she'd never felt before.

"Come on," she said, putting her shoulder under his arm and reaching around his back to support him. "I'll carry you home."

He laughed and they walked up the trail together. When they reached the main path, they turned left. Brian stopped and took her face into both his hands. "I'm having a great time." He kissed her. "And it's only Saturday. We have the rest of the weekend to enjoy each other's company."

"It might take that long for you to recover!" she teased. "But don't worry—"

A movement caught her eye. She looked past Brian, her face changing from love to horror. Brian, seeing her expression, spun around to follow her gaze. Suzanne put her hand up to her mouth and stifled a scream.

Sam Carlucci, her ex-husband, the man who was supposed to be in jail, came walking down the sandy path toward them. In his right hand, he held an ugly black pistol.

"Well, well, what do we have here," he said. "Looks like a nature walk at the nudist colony."

Suzanne suddenly felt very exposed. Instinctively, she covered her groin.

Sam laughed. "Hey! What's the matter? You know how many times I saw you naked? How many times we made love? Don't get shy on me now or I'm liable to demand my marital rights, if ya know what I mean."

Brian's head swiveled around to Suzanne. "You know him?"

She grimaced, her heart in her stomach. "My ex. Sam." She turned her fury on him. "What the hell are you doing here? Why aren't you in prison?"

"It was jail, sweet-cheeks. You should know—you put me there." He cocked his head. "They let me out early for good behavior." His grin widened. "Didn't they tell you?"

Suzanne had never felt so angry in her life. Angry and scared. "No, they didn't. What do you want with us?"

"What's the matter? Can't I come in and join your little nudist colony? Maybe Armstrong and I could compare notes, hmmm? How was she in the sack, *Brian*?"

So, Suzanne thought, *he clearly knows who Brian is, which means he's been following me for a while. What the hell is he up to?*

"Don't be shy, hon. Let me see all of you." He wiggled the gun at her hand covering herself.

Reluctantly, Suzanne took it away. Sam's eyes fell onto her little lightning bolt and burst out laughing. Suzanne flushed red from her breasts to her cheeks.

"Dammit, gal, you really put on a show! Did Armstrong make you do that? Or was that your own idea?"

Suzanne said nothing. She just stood there, tears running down her face, humiliated beyond endurance.

"Listen, asshole—" Brian took a step toward him, but Sam backed up, forcing Brian to stop in his tracks.

"Uh-huh. That's close enough." He turned back to Suzanne. "That's rich. I mean to tell you. If you'd done some cute things like that for me, why, we'd probably never have gotten divorced." He waggled the gun at them. "Now, let's go see your little love shack." He forced them to turn and head up the path toward the cabin, making sure he stayed well out of Brian's reach.

Suzanne could feel Brian's eyes on her like a great weight. Just when she had been the happiest she'd been in months, Sam had to return to snatch it away.

"Look, I didn't know he was out," she tried to explain, talking out of the side of her mouth, hoping Sam wouldn't hear.

Brian held up a hand. "It's okay." He seemed coldly furious again and Suzanne could see his mind working, trying to figure out how to get them out of this situation. They reached the house in minutes. At the door, they turned, waiting for directions from Sam. Brian seemed tense, like a coiled spring. She thought, *if Sam gets just a little too close…*

Sam apparently caught his body language. "Oh, and if you're thinking I'm going to give you a chance to jump me, forget it. I know all about what you did the other night, that Jackie Chan shit."

Suzanne, who thought she couldn't be more surprised, was rocked further. "You! You set those thugs on us!"

"Yeah, and it's a good thing I did! I might've made a mistake getting too close to your lover here." He waved the gun at Brian. "You've got some moves, don't cha? And not just in the sack." He winked at Suzanne. "Mister, if you want to stay alive, you'll not come any closer to me than you are right now. I see you so much as take a step toward me, and I'll kill you. Inside."

Tears began to flow from Suzanne's eyes as they entered the sliding glass door into the kitchen. Sam was ruining everything. What had happened to the man she had married so many years ago? This madman with a gun seemed a stranger.

She turned on him in sudden fury. "Why are you doing this, Sam? What the hell's gotten into you?"

His anger flared for the first time. "You have to ask, after having me tossed into jail!"

"You stalked me! You slashed my tires! You punched me!"

"You didn't have to file charges. You could've talked to me about it. I would've paid for the damn tires. I said I was sorry I hit you. Instead, you ruined my life."

Suzanne let her anger boil over. "How can you say that? All I wanted was to be left alone! You did it to yourself!" She took a step toward him.

Sam waved the gun, forcing her to back off. "I lost my job, and now it's gonna be tough to get another one—all because you chose to take the hard road. Well, honey bun, the hard road has come full circle."

Brian couldn't believe what he was seeing and hearing. *How could this sweet, demure, wonderful woman ever have been married to this complete idiot? And how did this man follow us to the island? And, more to the point, why? Does he intend to kill us in order to get even with his ex-wife? Am I going to end up an innocent victim, a guy in the wrong place at the wrong time?*

His mind raced, trying to find a way to close the gap between them. When Sam told him he had been responsible for those two thugs, his heart fell. The element of surprise was lost. He had little chance against a gun if he couldn't close the distance between them.

If Sam wanted revenge, he could just shoot them where they stood and there was little Brian could do about it, other than to charge him and hope that the first bullet didn't kill him. Slim chance there. Being nude didn't help his chances, either.

"What do you want? Revenge?" he said, trying to keep his voice from betraying his intense anger.

"Revenge?" Sam nodded. "Yeah. I want some revenge. How about getting seven months of my life back?"

"Seven months? That's all you were in jail?" Brian couldn't believe it. "You're risking a life sentence right now. Why not take the seven months as an object lesson and move on?"

Brian's words seemed to hit home. "Shut up." Then to Suzanne, "I had to pay you back somehow and I wasn't sure how to do it. I mean, killing you would be too easy. I wanted to ruin you. But when you started dating this rich guy, I got another idea. A way you can pay me back."

Brian sensed an opening. He thought Sam just wanted to kill them, but if it was money he wanted, perhaps they could survive this insane man.

"What do you mean, pay you back?" Suzanne asked, her face set.

"Well, the way I figure it, you owe me about a year's salary, plus future earnings until I get another job." His voice darkened. "Which is gonna be hard now that I have a record, thanks to you."

"You want money? That's what this kidnapping is about?" Brian used the word on purpose, to startle Sam and to let him know how serious the crime had become.

"Kidnapping? Hell, I'm just visiting two naked lovebirds. I haven't kidnapped anyone."

"Then you won't mind if we leave," Brian said and made to take Suzanne's arm and turn away.

"I wouldn't if I were you." The gun centered on his chest, forcing him to stand still. "Okay, you're right. *Now* it's kidnapping," Sam laughed, an evil sound that echoed in the small kitchen. "Now sit down and shut up." He pointed at the kitchen chairs.

With no alternative, they sat.

Sam dumped his bag onto the counter next to him. "Here's the deal, folks. You cooperate, and you'll live. You try anything and you both die."

Suzanne and Brian exchanged worried glances and turned their attention back to Sam.

"Okay. It's very simple. I want two hundred grand. I figure your boyfriend's good for it and you can pay him back in trade." He gave that creepy laugh again.

"I don't have that kind of money here," Brian pointed out.

His anger flared up. "I know that! You think I'm a dummy?" He took a breath, as if steadying himself. "No, this is how it's gonna play out. My ex stays here, keeping the home fires burning, while Armstrong and I go to a bank. There's one up the road."

Brian tried to think of roadblocks to throw up at his plan. It sounded crazy to him. "I can't get two hundred thousand dollars. Not unless I sell some securities and I can't—it's Saturday."

Sam's eyes narrowed. "You'd better think of a way and real quick." He pulled some handcuffs out of the bag. "Here." He tossed them to Suzanne who caught them in both hands, eyes wide. "Go put them on your boyfriend, arms behind his back."

Suzanne rose, shakily, and moved around behind Brian. He brought his hands together for her. "I'm sorry," she said, tears, flowing down her cheeks, as she snapped them around his wrists. "I'm so sorry."

"Not too tight—we wouldn't want him to lose the circulation in his hands. He'll have to sign some documents I'm sure."

Brian knew the odds were diminishing fast. He could still kick the gun out of his hand, but it would be much harder without the use of his hands, and could lead to both their deaths. He decided to wait it out, look for an opening.

Sam seemed to relax, now that Brian was cuffed. "Now we get to the good part." He reached into the bag and pulled out a length of rope then a chain, with an object about a foot-long duct-taped in the center. It rattled ominously as he held it up.

"What the hell is that?" Brian asked.

"What does it look like?"

Brian peered at it. There was a long round cylinder, red at each end where it stuck out from the duct tape and a small red light shining through a hole cut in the tape. The object had been taped right in the center of the length of chain. He was afraid that he knew exactly what it was.

"Now I can't trust Suzie here to simply wait patiently while we're gone. Nor can I trust Brian to behave himself. So I brought along a little protection." He pointed the gun at Suzanne. "Stand up."

Slowly, she stood, shaking. Brian watched intently every move Sam made. *Just give me an opening,* he begged silently. *Come on!*

Sam approached Suzanne from behind, keeping her in between him and Brian. He bent down and put the gun on the floor next to him, then pulled the chain tight around her waist, above her hips. Suzanne gasped. "Ow!"

"Relax, baby. This has gotta be tight. Can't have you slipping out of it."

Brian tried to edge to the side, thinking he might be able to charge him, knock him away from his gun. But the man was too quick. Like a snake, he snatched up the pistol and leveled it at Suzanne's head. "Don't," he warned. Brian sank back in his chair.

Sam put the gun down again, threaded a padlock through the links in back and locked it. He took the section of rope and tied her hands behind her, then used more rope to fasten her naked body to the wooden chair, ignoring her grunts when he jerked the knots tight. He picked up the gun and stepped back.

Brian cursed inwardly. Sam had never given him a chance to move.

"This little device is my insurance policy," Sam said, moving back toward the gym bag. He pulled out a small electronic device, about the size of a transistor radio. "This here is a powerful transmitter, guaranteed to go five miles.

That's good, you see, because that bank is about four miles from here."

Brian was beginning to understand what Sam was up to.

"Suzie, what I put around your waist is a stick of dynamite, wired to a receiver."

Suzanne jerked, her eyes wide. "You bastard!"

"Here's how it's going to play out," his voice was hard. He held up the transmitter. Both Suzanne and Brian could see the small green light glowing on the front of it. "Boyfriend and I are going off in the boat, leaving you to think about what might go wrong, say if he does something foolish."

Sam turned philosophical. "Now, the truth is, I wanted to get a few sticks of dynamite, so it'd be quick and painless, but it turned out to be harder than I thought to get my hands on some. So with one stick, I figured it'll just blow a good-sized hole in you. Might not kill you right off the bat. You'll just lie here and bleed to death."

He looked meaningfully at Brian. "All I gotta do is push this button," he showed the small knob at the top of the device, next to the antenna. "I'm going to carry this in my left hand the whole way and back. You do what I say, and she lives. You screw it up, or you try to cheat me out of my money, and…blam!" He jerked his hand, causing both Brian and Suzanne to react.

He laughed again.

Brian thought fast. He didn't think he could raise two hundred thousand, but Sam clearly wasn't going to take no for an answer. He knew he had about sixty thousand in his bank. Where could he get the rest?

"Sam." He tried to level with him. Maybe he'd listen to reason. "Sam, I told you, I don't have two hundred thousand I can get today. If you give me until Monday, I can raise—"

"Shut up!" Sam screamed at him. He held up the box. "How 'bout if we step outside and I'll blow her up right now? You can listen to her screams as I shoot you four, five times."

Shit! "All right! All right! I can probably borrow the money. But that's going to take time and it might raise suspicion."

Sam said ominously, "You'd better come up with a good explanation, 'cause right now, I don't really care whether you both live or die. You get me my money, I'll walk away. You'll never see me again."

"You can't get away with this!" Suzanne cried. "Where will you go? The police will find you!"

"Don't worry, I got a plan."

Brian feared that plan might involve their deaths.

Chapter Twenty-Five

Sam was loving this. He had his ex and her new honey so scared they were ready to wet their pants. Only Suzie wasn't wearing any. He loved seeing her naked again. Reminded him of the good days, when they were first married. Boy, that cunt couldn't get enough of him! And what's up with that razor job? He'd never seen anything like that in his life. It still caused him a chuckle.

He could tell they completely bought his story about the dynamite. What a couple of chumps! It probably would've taken him a week or more to track down some explosives. But a forty-nine cent road flare with a Radio Shack light attached to a battery was all he needed. Cover it up with duct tape and viola! Instant "bomb".

The "transmitter" he held was simply the same radio receiver he'd used when he bugged Suzanne's apartment. He used black electrician's tape to cover over the words that might give away the secret, especially the ones near the button on the top that said "A, B Freq." It allowed you to place two bugs and switch between them. But to these idiots, it looked just like a detonator button.

He loved it that Suzanne was going to sweat here, buck naked, thinking she might be blow up at any second while they were gone for hours. These few hours of terror don't begin to make up for his own terrible experiences in jail, but it was a start. The money would help too. His asshole clenched at the memory of the three big black men holding him down while they assaulted him. He couldn't do a god-damned thing about it. He couldn't squeal and he couldn't escape. They had owned him from that moment on.

Revenge would be sweet. His real treat would come after they returned. There was no way he'd leave witnesses. He planned to stage a murder-suicide, and then slip away on his boat with the money. The police would be baffled. They might wonder why Armstrong took the money out of the bank, but with no evidence that anyone else was on the island, they'd have to close the case.

Sam would walk away a free man. He figured he could live like a king in Mexico on two hundred thou for a few years. Then, when it was time, he could look into something else just as lucrative as today's job. Bank robberies, for example. He'd learned a lot in jail.

He grabbed the empty gym bag and pointed the gun at the tycoon. "Let's go."

"You plan to walk me into a bank naked, with my hands in cuffs?"

"Relax. I'll let you get dressed. And you'll walk into the bank a free man. Just remember—I'll have the transmitter in my left hand at all times. You try anything funny, I kill your little Lightnin' Bolt. Got it?"

Brian nodded, his eyes boring holes into him. Sam ignored this useless display of temper. He had him by the balls and he wasn't about to let go.

"Okay, let's get you some clothes. I'm tired of looking at your little weenie."

He forced Brian upstairs, where he pulled a pair of shorts and a T-shirt from the suitcase and tossed them onto the bed. He made Brian stand on the other side, while Sam stayed by the door. He tossed the handcuff key onto the bed in front of him. "Now, uncuff yourself, put on your clothes and lie down on the bed on your stomach."

* * * * *

Brian could see Sam was not going to give him an opening. With that damned transmitter in one hand, he had no choice but to comply. He turned around and picked up the key, then fumbled around blindly until he felt it slide home. With a quick twist, the handcuff fell from his left wrist. He started to undo the other side but Sam shook his head. "You won't have them loose long enough to bother with that. Drop the key on the bed and get dressed."

Brian was at least grateful to no longer be naked in front of Suzanne's ex-husband. It just felt too creepy. Once he had his clothes on, he lay on the bed, as he'd been ordered.

Sam crept close and quickly fastened the loose cuff onto his wrist. Brian didn't move. Sam moved back and told him to get up.

"You got wallet, ID, keys to the truck?"

Brian nodded. "Downstairs."

Sam led him back into the kitchen. "Honey, Brian and I have to go out for a little while. Are you sure you'll be okay here? You need anything while we're out?" He laughed. Suzanne turned her head away.

Sam picked up Brian's keys and wallet then jerked his head toward the door. "Let's go."

Sam moved well back, out of reach and kept the gun on him. He waggled the pistol, indicating Brian should go first. Sighing to himself, Brian moved toward the open door.

"See ya, honey," Sam told Suzanne. "Hope you don't get too cold here, sitting naked, waiting to find out if you live or die." He shot her a wolfish grin and pushed Brian out the door. Brian could hear Suzanne's sobs behind him. His heart ached.

Sam stayed a good five feet back as they walked down to the dock. Brian was forced into the bow while Sam untied the lines. He jumped in and cranked up the motor. In seconds, they were headed to shore.

Brian looked around carefully, hoping to spot a fisherman or maybe someone taking a walk on the shore, but they arrived without being seen. Sam jumped out at the dock and quickly tied up the boat. Brian had some trouble getting out of the bobbing craft with his hands behind him, but Sam refused to help. He just waited for him a few feet away, gun leveled, looking around for strangers.

They made it to the truck. Sam unlocked the passenger side and stepped back while Brian struggled in. He went around to the driver's side and slid in behind the wheel. Brian could tell he was uncomfortable, being this close to him. That told him this creep was afraid of him.

"Don't you try anything while we're driving," Sam warned, holding up the fake transmitter. "You so much as twitch, and I'll blow her up, I swear it."

Brian nodded his eyes steady on him. He prayed for just two seconds free of his cuffs and with that transmitter out of Sam's hands. Just two seconds. He'd risk the gun, but he couldn't risk Suzanne.

They drove through the dappled trees until they hit the highway, then Sam turned toward the town of Kelseyville, just four miles away. He stopped at the first bank they came to and parked in a corner of the lot, within sight of the front door. Brian looked out, thinking how quiet, how normal the scene seemed to be—people walking, going about their Saturday errands, while just a few yards away, he was a prisoner to a madman.

"Don't move." Sam got out and climbed into the backseat. "Put your arms over the back of the seat."

Brian had to lean forward. With much difficulty, he managed to hook his arms over the seat. Sam pressed the gun between his shoulder blades. He tossed Brian's wallet and the empty gym bag on the seat next to the man.

"Here's the deal. You go in, ask for the manager, tell him you want the money. I'll come in a few seconds behind you. If I suspect you've told anyone what's going on, I blow up Suzie, shoot you, and maybe a few others, and take off."

"You'll be caught."

"Maybe so. But she'll be dead. And that'll be your last thought on this Earth."

Brian nodded. "I'll cooperate. Just don't push that button!"

Sam's wicked laugh rang in his ears. "Say please."

Brian gritted his teeth, thinking how he'd love to take this man apart. "Please," he rumbled.

Sam unlocked the cuffs. Brian brought his wrists around to rub the circulation back into them. He was stalling and he knew it.

"Go," Sam ordered.

Brian knew he couldn't reach around behind him in time to prevent Sam from detonating the bomb. He got out and headed into the bank.

* * * * *

Suzanne struggled against the ropes, twisting and turning her wrists, trying to pull the knot loose enough to slip a hand out. *Dammit! Why did Sam have to show up now, here? Why can't I ever be rid of him?*

She feared Sam would kill them. That's the only way he could get away. She thought about Brian being held at gunpoint. She knew he was capable of defending himself, but with this damn bomb on her, he's helpless.

If I can only get my hands free, maybe I can disarm it.

She struggled, tears clouding her vision. She couldn't believe her luck. It just wasn't fair. Far beyond her own feelings of helplessness was her concern for Brian. She just had to do something to help! She twisted her wrist again and felt the ropes bite into her.

Stop! Stop! her mind told her. *Relax.* Don't force anything. She tried to visualize the knots, the way Sam had tied them. He had looped the rope around her waist, tying her to the chair then tied her wrists, before tying more rope to the chair. It was all one big rope. So theoretically, slack somewhere else could be transferred to the knots on her wrists if she could untie the right knots.

Struggling against the knots on her wrists was counterproductive, she realized. It would only tighten them. However, when Sam had forced her back against the chair, she had cupped her shoulder blades, adding some slack to the rope. If she was lucky, very lucky, she might be able to use that bit of slack.

She reached up with her left hand and found the knot that tied her to the chair. It was a simple double knot. Digging her fingernails into it, she worked to loosen it. A fingernail snapped off, causing sudden pain to her finger. She gasped, but went right back at it.

After several minutes of intense work, Suzanne felt the knot slip loose and wanted to shout with relief. It had taken far too long. The ropes slackened across her chest and she wiggled her arms, trying to bring the slack back to her wrists. Drawing a deep, calming breath, she visualized the ropes leading into the knots. Grabbing the rope next to the knot, she pushed it forward, into the tangle. With her other hand, she awkwardly reached up and tugged at one loop of the coiled knot.

It took several minutes of seesawing back and forth, pushing a little, tugging a little, until she felt the knot loosen. She pulled hard and it came free. There was another knot underneath, so she repeated the process, looking out the window occasionally at the empty dock, hoping she'd have enough time.

*****

Brian thought through all the parameters as he entered the bank. He could tell the manager what was going on, and ask him not to call the police until they left. But the police would have to show up somewhere. If Sam saw a cop, he'd probably trigger the bomb just for spite.

The guy is completely nuts, he thought. He spends—what?—less than a year in jail and he's ready to throw away the rest of his life? Does he really think a lousy two hundred grand is going to be worth the trouble he's getting into? Does he really hate his ex-wife that much?

Brian decided to play it straight. He'd get the money somehow, then look for an opportunity to take down Sam. He had no illusions that the man intended to let them live. They'd have police on his ass before he could get out of the county. No, the way Brian figured it, Sam would kill them and hide their bodies. With luck, no one would notice they were missing for days, maybe weeks. The police might even think they drowned in the lake.

He approached the manager, who introduced himself as Bob Pritchert. "I have an opportunity to buy some rare antiques, but I need to get some money out of my personal account at another bank and my business account," he explained.

Pritchert raised his eyebrows, but after Brian showed him his I.D., he became much more cooperative. Getting the money out of his account was no problem, but it took considerable doing to obtain the money from Armstrong Control Systems. After all, he was stealing it.

While he negotiated with Pritchert, Brian noticed Sam stroll in and stand at the counter, pretending to fill out a deposit slip. Brian tried to ignore him. The last thing he wanted to do was spook him now. He believed his threat to kill Suzanne and shoot up the bank.

Brian had to call his CFO, Bill Hangstrom, at home to get the necessary funds released from the corporate account. Hangstrom had a dozen questions, but Brian cut him off with a blunt, "I'll explain later," and managed to convince him of the urgency of the situation without revealing details. He knew he had a lot of explaining to do Monday.

Hell, by Monday, he might be dead.

Forty minutes after he entered the bank, Brian walked out with a gym bag full of hundreds, fifties and twenties. Two hundred thousand, in cash.

Sam stood by the SUV, waiting for him. Brian thought he might have a chance to jump him while his arms were still free, but Sam climbed into the backseat long before he could reach the car. He held up the transmitter so Brian could see it.

"Get in," he growled, indicating he should sit in the passenger seat. Brian cooperated, seething at the missed opportunity. "Put the bag down and bring your hands back over the seat. Don't try anything."

Sighing, he brought his hands over and let Sam refasten the cuffs. The man was just too careful.

Sam came around to the front and got in behind the wheel. He picked up the bag, hefting it. "You got it all?"

Brian nodded.

Sam grinned and started the car. "Good. Now let's get you back to your dear sweetheart."

Brian sat quietly as they drove, imagining all the possibilities for escape. Unfortunately, every scenario he could come up with, the transmitter stymied him. He couldn't afford to make a mistake that might cause Sam to trigger the bomb. He'd never forgive himself if anything happened to Suzanne.

Of all the women he'd dated in the last two months, she stood out by far. She had the right combination of brains, beauty and a sense of herself that didn't require her to one-up men. He thought she would enjoy being "kept" without it becoming a cage. Nor did she seem the type who would become greedy and demanding.

In short, she had seemed like the perfect foil to his forceful personality—except for this one small problem—a violent and insane ex-husband.

They made it to the boat without incident. Brian got in front and Sam started up the motor for the return trip. He heard his captor chuckling to himself behind him. He worried about how Suzanne was handling being tied up to a bomb, fearful it might go off at any minute.

Chapter Twenty-Six

Suzanne finally got the last knot loose and quickly untied her ankles. Her fingers were bloody and pinched, but she was free. She stood and stared at the chain around her waist. She felt the padlock behind her. She'd never get that off, not without the key. She tried to slip it over her hips, but Sam had cinched it in tight.

Shaking, she knew she had only one chance left. To disarm it. If she made a mistake, she'd be blown up and it wouldn't matter if Brian had managed to overpower Sam. He'd return to find her bloody body on the floor and blame himself for it.

Suzanne bent down and began picking at the edges of the tape, trying to sneak into it, like someone might try to open a letter without anyone being able to tell. Her hands shook and she tried not to think about it blowing up in her face.

She doubted the bomb would be too sophisticated—that wasn't Sam's style. It might be as simple as unhooking a wire. She peeled back a section of tape and found herself staring at writing on one side of the red cylinder—*Caution: Point End Away from Face.* What the hell? She peeled a bit more tape, being careful not to jar the bomb, which she now had strong suspicions about. Four more words came into view—*Road Safety Highway Flare.*

As her mouth dropped open in surprise, she heard the sound of a motorboat approaching.

* * * * *

They pulled up to the dock and Sam jumped out, the gym bag slung diagonally around his chest. He tied off the boat and helped Armstrong climb out. He couldn't stop smiling—he was in a very good mood all of a sudden.

"You go first," he said, pointing the gun at the man, jerking his head toward the house.

Shoulders sagging, Brian walked to the sliding glass door, then waited for Sam to open it, his hands still cuffed behind him. Sam stepped around him and slid it open, and waved him in. As he came in behind him, he saw that Suzanne had turned herself around, so her naked back faced the door. Ropes still criss-crossed her back and appeared to be tied around her wrists.

"Whassa matter, Suzie—afraid someone will see you buck nekked?" He laughed, then pushed Armstrong to the side and approached her.

Wait. *What's that?* There was something wrong with the way she was sitting, he thought. No, there's something resting between her legs, isn't there? Something that wasn't there before?

The gun, which had been pointing in Armstrong's direction, began to swivel toward her when she suddenly jumped up, grabbed a small oar that had been resting between her legs and swung it hard down on his wrist.

He screamed as the pain rocketed up his arm. The gun flew out of his grasp and skittered across the tiled floor. Instantly, he dived for it when he heard Suzanne shout, *"The bomb's a fake!"*

Oh shit, Sam thought.

* * * * *

Brian's heart leapt when he saw Suzanne had somehow freed herself and struck at Sam's arm with the paddle. But he feared that he'd activate the bomb, and in these close quarters, they'd all be injured or killed.

Then he heard Suzanne shout, *"The bomb's a fake!"* and saw Sam go for the gun. He reacted instantly, without thought. His right foot came up, catching Sam's face as he lunged for the floor, crushing his nose and snapping his head back.

Sam recoiled, blood on his mouth, then tried again, coming in with a crab-like move sideways to protect his face, ducking down for the gun. His hand scrabbled across the smooth tiles.

If he gets that gun, we're all dead, Brian thought.

His left foot kicked out, catching Sam at the side of the knee, buckling it and eliciting another scream from the wounded man. He fell down and Brian managed to scoot in and kick the gun aside. It bounced up against the wall and careened off in another direction.

Now Suzanne jumped in with the oar, clubbing Sam about the head and shoulders. If it wasn't such a serious situation, it might've been comical—a stark naked woman, ropes still hanging from her body, pummeling her ex-husband over the back and head like a woman possessed.

"Get the gun!" Brian shouted, feeling helpless with his arms trapped behind him.

Suzanne looked up, her face a savage mask then her civilized self seemed to return. She scrambled past her groaning ex and picked up the pistol.

"The keys are in his pocket." Brian held the cuffs away from his body.

Nodding, she leveled the gun at Sam. "Sam, toss the keys over here."

"Fuck you!" he spat, blood dribbling down onto the floor. His face was a mask of pain and fury.

The gunshot was loud in the small room. Brian jumped, thinking she'd killed him, but she'd just fired a warning shot into his leg.

"Ow! Jesus! Stop! Stop it!" He reached into pocket and yanked out the keys, and slid them across the floor toward her.

"Wow," Brian said, completely taken with this tough, beautiful, together woman, standing naked, lightning bolt ablaze, the gun steady in both hands. "Remind me never to get on your bad side."

Grinning, she stooped down and picked up the handcuff keys. In seconds, Brian was free. He rubbed his wrists.

"Thanks for saving us."

"Couldn't've done it without you," she replied.

He swept her into his arms, taking the gun gently from her hand. "Now, before we get the sheriff out here, maybe you'd like to get dressed?"

Chapter Twenty-Seven

Two Sheriff's deputies and two detectives spent more than an hour on the island, questioning Brian and Suzanne after Sam had been taken away in the lake patrol boat, moaning and cursing the entire time.

Suzanne huddled in Brian's arms, the shock finally setting in. She couldn't stop hugging herself though she wasn't cold. She had put on shorts and a T-shirt, but she still felt exposed somehow. The detectives had offered to take them the hospital for a checkup, but they said they felt fine, just a little bruised and shaken.

They sat on the couch in the living room, with the two detectives across from them. One deputy hung around in the background, trying to look serious, while another one patrolled around outside, checking to make sure Sam had acted alone.

Brian and Suzanne told their story several times before the detectives were satisfied. They didn't tell the cops that Suzanne had shot Sam while he was already on the ground, defeated. They simply said he'd been shot during the struggle for the weapon. They doubted the cops would believe anything Sam told them. He'd be heading for prison this time, not the county jail.

Like Brian, the detectives were mystified as to why Sam would risk life in prison for a lousy two hundred grand. Suzanne offered insight into Sam's personality.

"It wasn't the money. It was the chance to put me down, to show that I made a mistake in rejecting him," she said, her voice pitched low. "He probably would've killed us both. Only then would he think he'd won."

Brian concurred with that assessment. "I couldn't figure out how he'd get away with it otherwise," he told them. "He couldn't let us live. My guess is he'd try to stage a murder-suicide, not that it would ever hold up. After all, I'm sure you cops would wonder where the money went."

Finally, the detectives seemed satisfied. They piled into the Sheriff's boat and headed away, leaving the couple alone. Brian and Suzanne stood near the dock, watching them recede in the distance, deep in thought.

"What do you say we leave our little paradise?" Brian offered.

"He ruined it, didn't he? I'm not sure we can ever look at this place the same way," she replied, her voice touched with sadness.

"Yeah. Maybe in time..." He let the thought hang. "Well, come on, let's pack up."

All those clothes that Suzanne had brought, all those sexy outfits, all those plans Brian had made, all the lovemaking they'd planned to do, all washed away by an embittered, insane, jealous ex-husband.

"I'll bet you're wondering what I ever saw in him," she said as they packed in the bedroom, suitcases open on the bed.

"The thought did occur to me. He seemed a bit rabid."

"He wasn't always that way. When we first got together, he was sweet and funny and, well, he looked out for me. It was only after we married that he changed. I think jealousy made him crazy."

"Jealousy? He thought you were going out with other men?"

"Constantly. He couldn't stand to have anyone even smile in my direction. He accused me of affairs with my mechanic, a meter man—even his brother."

"How long were you married?"

"Only about four years. I had to get out after that."

Silence fell as each tended to their own thoughts and their own packing. Suzanne could tell something was bothering him and it wasn't Sam. She let him wrestle with it. Finally, Brian stopped, and turned to her. "Well, I feel pretty foolish, right about now."

"Why? What do you mean?"

"Come on. I advertise for a 'kept woman', thinking I'm going to get some cute little lady who won't ever challenge me or argue with me—just do everything I wanted. You know, the 'perfect woman'." He made quote marks in the air. "But that's not what you are at all. You are an amazing woman—tough, tenacious, witty, sexy—you're certainly no demure little pushover."

"I don't think of myself as tough. Just a survivor. But it was more than that. I felt responsible for Sam's being here. I felt like I had to fix it."

"You certainly did that. And in doing so, you just made me realize how silly my quest was. I'm like a sexist Don Quixote—searching for something that no longer exists. Furthermore, I realized it's not something I'd want. I mean, for just one obvious example, if you'd been waiting for me to save you today, we'd both be dead."

Suzanne nodded, embarrassed at the kind words. "Don't feel bad. I never would've answered the ad if it hadn't've reached me somehow, deep inside. I think women are looking for something that makes them feel safe, protected—'kept' in some sense of the word. At least I am."

"So we're both just slaves to our caveman—or woman—ancestry?"

She laughed. "Maybe that's it. Maybe part of me likes being a little bit of a sex object, at least under certain circumstances. Let you be the big hunter, bring me a mastodon to cook. I'll just wait here, naked by the fire, so you can ravish me after dinner."

"Yeah. I think that appeals to men on a basic level. We get to beat our chests and rule the roost." He stopped packing and took her into his arms.

"The problem is, that's not what I really want. I was blinded by the shallow, silly women I'd been meeting. The ones who feel a day at the mall is more important than a walk on the beach at sunset, or meeting a movie star is better than reading a good book."

Suzanne shrugged. "I guess I can understand that. Your value system got skewed. By placing that ad, you were trying to balance the scales somehow."

"Yeah. Boy was I wrong! But it worked out all right. I met you." She blushed then, a rose red that lit up her neck and face.

"You know, I really like the way you blush."

"That's good, 'cause I do it a lot."

Brian kissed her. She responded with more heat than she thought possible, considering the circumstances. They clung to each other, like two survivors.

The kiss lingered. He moved down to her neck, nibbling, making her giggle.

"I love you," he whispered. "And I want you."

It seemed incongruous, with their near-death experience so close behind them, but Suzanne felt the passion too. It welled up in her like a force, a need that could not be denied. No doubt, it was heightened by the emotional roller coaster they'd experienced that day. "I want you, too."

They fell together on the bed, kissing and touching. The suitcases flopped to the floor, spilling their contents. They didn't care. Their clothes fell away. Suzanne felt completely comfortable with Brian, as if they had seen each other naked for months or years, not hours.

She noticed a small scar on his chest, below his left shoulder and touched it, reminding herself to ask about it later. She wanted to know everything about this man. She had a feeling they would be together for a long time.

He kissed her hard, his tongue slipping in to caress hers. His hands slid up and down her body. Her breath became shallow.

Deep in her mind, a small, insignificant voice said, *Condom!*

Dammit! Shut up! We were nearly killed and you have to think about that?

She reached down and felt his cock hardening to its full length. She let her fingers dance over it, trying to memorize it like a blind woman might. It seemed perfect, just like Brian.

He reared up over her, his broad chest held up by his arms. His eyes looked deeply into hers. She could feel his cock just touching the entrance to her pussy. God, she wanted him so bad!

"Um," he said. She knew instantly what he was about to say.

"Condom," she said in a sigh.

He nodded, his face questioning hers.

It only took her a half-second to decide. "No, just fuck me, you big, bad man."

Epilogue

Suzanne sat by the pool, wearing a new white one-piece swimsuit stretched by her bulge in the middle, her browned body covered in suntan lotion and sweat. A large floppy hat and oversized sunglasses shaded her face. Wendy sat on the lounge beside her, dressed in a scandalous bikini.

"See, this is what I was talking about," Wendy said. "It's not so bad being 'kept', now is it?"

"No, it's not."

"Are you sure Brian doesn't have a brother?"

"Oh, stop. If he did, he'd probably have an ordinary job and you wouldn't be interested anyway. You want to have it all, Wen."

"You sure lucked out."

"Hey, I worked hard for this man! We nearly got killed, remember. I wouldn't've blamed him if he had walked out of my life forever."

"Yeah, well, this is all thanks to me, you know. You would never have applied if not for me. You could at least share."

"Now stop that! You'll have to find your own rich husband."

"Yeah, yeah. You always were selfish." She had an amused lilt in her voice.

"You were always the slutty one," Suzanne responded, grinning.

A comfortable silence descended again. Good friends don't need to fill the air with continuous conversation and Wendy was still her best friend, after Brian, of course. She debated whether it was time to turn to her other side or to go sit under the umbrella, perhaps have an iced tea. She selected a fourth choice. She rose, dropped her hat and glasses and dove into the pool, luxuriating as the cool water washed over her. Refreshed, she climbed out, smoothing her hair.

"Come on in and cool off. You look hot."

"What? And mess up my hair? No thanks." Wendy shook her head and lay back.

Checking the clock by the back door, Suzanne noted it was about five-thirty. Brian would be home soon. She loved Mondays. The maid always took the day off, leaving her alone in the big townhouse overlooking San Francisco. The pool was small, but very secluded.

It was seven months after their terrible ordeal with Sam. There were questions, depositions and, of course, the trial itself. Suzanne had been embarrassed to have Brian dragged into it, but he had seemed to take it well.

"Sure it's a hassle," he had told her. "But I look upon this like I would any other problem I had. 'The only way out is through,' so let's get it over with."

Fortunately, the trial didn't take long. Sam had been convicted and sentenced to twenty-five years in prison. His defense attorney had used Sam's rape in jail in an attempt to mitigate his actions, saying he wasn't responsible, that he'd gone temporarily insane. The jury didn't buy it. But at least Suzanne and Brian had a better understanding as to what had driven Sam's quest for revenge.

The lust they had felt for each other had not diminished with time. If anything, it had deepened, mellowed and turned into love. Suzanne didn't think love was possible again after Sam. But Brian coaxed her along, letting her know he would take this journey with her.

Suzanne reflected on how much her life had changed in the past few months. She truly was a kept woman, she decided—in the best sense of the word. Brian kept her in clothes, in good foods and wines, in beautiful homes and in love.

In turn, she kept Brian happy and relaxed. She fulfilled his every wish, just by being herself.

If this was what being a kept woman was all about, bring on the leg irons, she thought, a statement she had made more than once to Brian.

She heard the sliding glass door and turned to see Brian come out, still dressed in his dark slacks, shirt and tie, his sport coat slung over his shoulder.

"Wow, what a sight for sore eyes." Wendy couldn't help but flirt.

"Oh, hush. You can't have him."

"Pshaw."

"Hi, Wendy. Good to see you again." Brian's eyes, however, never left Suzanne.

Wendy looked from Brian to Suzanne. "Well, it looks like I'd better go home before I get burned up by all the sparks you two are shooting at each other."

"Huh? Oh, okay. Thanks for coming by." Suzanne stood and came into Brian's arms.

Wendy got up and gathered her things. "Don't worry, I'll see myself out. I've got a hot date tonight anyway—with some guy named Duracell."

Neither one seemed to be paying attention. Wendy laughed and shook her head, then walked up the steps and disappeared inside.

"Hey, honey. I was just thinking about you," she said, giving him a fierce hug. Brian didn't seem to care that she was getting his clothes wet.

"Come on in, I'd like to change clothes."

"Sure. Me too."

They went inside, where the air was cooler and headed for the bedroom. Suzanne stripped off her swimsuit and jumped into the shower. Brian joined her a few seconds later and they giggled like kids and washed each other off.

With the water pounding on their backs, Brian pressed Suzanne up against the tiles and ran his fingers suggestively over her lightning bolt. The silly little affectation had become a private joke between them, and Brian clearly enjoyed the look, so Suzanne had kept it neatly trimmed, just for him. Their little secret.

"God, I'd love to hang around here with you all day," he said, running his hands over her swollen stomach.

"Well, somebody's got to earn the money, so I can relax by the pool," she teased. "Of course, I could always go get my job back. I'm sure Jack would take me in. I might have to blow him or something, but…"

He hugged her gently until she stopped talking. He let her go and stepped back, eyeing her up and down. Then he turned off the taps and helped his pregnant wife out, making sure she didn't slip. He handed her a towel.

"I can see I'm doing a lousy job of making you my subservient little woman," he said. "You lie around her all day, naked all the time, probably masturbating up a storm, and I'll bet you haven't done any cleaning."

She hit him on the arm, a light slap. "Oh shush. You've got Maria for that. Why, I might break a nail," she teased.

He grinned. "I have to admit, I like Mondays the best. I never know what I'm going to find when I come home. I think about you a lot during the day, swimming or exercising, maybe being naked and sweaty…"

"You like the way I look?" She was fishing. "I've gained a little weight, you know." She patted her stomach.

"You know I do." He put his hand on hers over her swelling body. They stood together for a moment, feeling the life within. Suzanne felt Brian's cock rise against her bare thigh.

"Well, maybe we don't need Maria *every* day. Maybe she could take Fridays off too. I mean, until…"

"Ohh. That'd be nice. I'd like to come home for the weekend, knowing that you'll be here just waiting for me, all hot and bothered."

"I'm hot all right. Hot flashes. I could use a little lovin' right about now. That always seems to calm me down. Just watch out for junior."

"Hey, remember, I'm supposed to be the boss! I'll tell you when you'll get a little lovin'."

"Okay." She turned away and grabbed up the towel, covering herself. "I guess I'll start making your dinner, master!"

He grabbed her by the arm before she could escape. "Wait. I think I'm ready now." She looked down to see him swelling to his full glory.

She rolled up into his arms. "Are you sure?" She touched him, causing his cock to harden further.

Brian took the towel away from her and let it drop on the floor. "Oh, I'm sure."

He pulled her into the bedroom.

Enjoy this excerpt from

The Cameo

Dorothy Eckland was every bit the professional woman. At least that was how she saw herself. Her chin was raised a little higher and her shoulders held more erect as she walked among the common folk.

Dorothy worked as a loan officer at a downtown bank, where image was important. She dressed impeccably and usually wore her dark blonde hair up in a bun. She had a no-nonsense attitude about her life and the people in it. Rules helped define her existence. She obeyed bank regulations at work, traffic regulations on the streets and her own moral code otherwise.

At twenty-eight, she was in the prime of her life. She was good-looking, reasonably well to do and respected. Dorothy might admit to herself that she was lonely on occasion, but she'd usually dismiss it by telling herself how lucky she was.

Dorothy had a routine she followed. Every day, sharp at nine, she'd show up at the bank, settle into her desk along the back wall and start her paperwork from the previous day. Other employees would nod at her, just to be polite—she rarely participated in office chitchat. Customers would come in, hats in hand, obsequiously looking for loans, and Dorothy would handle them with measured compassion, even though in a secret part of her, she found them too needy and desperate.

At 11:30, she'd get the nod from the balding, officious bank manager, Mr. Darkin. She'd rise, take her purse from the bottom drawer of her desk and head out for lunch. Other employees knew not to ask her to join them—she'd refused too many times before. Privacy was a protected asset. She usually ate at the restaurant across the street, then spent some time walking through the park down the block if the weather was nice. If it rained, she might stop at the library or run a few quick errands.

At precisely five o'clock, when the heavy bank doors shut, she'd gather her things, nod goodbye to the other officers and to Mr. Darkin, then head home on the subway to her one-bedroom apartment. She had no cat, no dog, no goldfish. She liked it that way. Her life was well organized and efficient.

On Thursday, the second day of May, Dorothy's ordered existence took a sharp detour.

About the author:

J.W. McKenna is a former journalist who took up penning erotic romance stories after years of trying to ignore an overly dramatic—and often overheated—imagination. McKenna is married and lives in the Midwest, where polite people would be shocked if they knew what kind of writing was being done in their town.

J.W. McKenna welcomes mail from readers. You can write to her c/o Ellora's Cave Publishing at 1056 Home Avenue, Akron OH 44310-3502.

Why an electronic book?

We live in the Information Age—an exciting time in the history of human civilization in which technology rules supreme and continues to progress in leaps and bounds every minute of every hour of every day. For a multitude of reasons, more and more avid literary fans are opting to purchase e-books instead of paperbacks. The question to those not yet initiated to the world of electronic reading is simply: *why?*

1. *Price.* An electronic title at Ellora's Cave Publishing runs anywhere from 40-75% less than the cover price of the exact same title in paperback format. Why? Cold mathematics. It is less expensive to publish an e-book than it is to publish a paperback, so the savings are passed along to the consumer.
2. *Space.* Running out of room to house your paperback books? That is one worry you will never have with electronic novels. For a low one-time cost, you can purchase a handheld computer designed specifically for e-reading purposes. Many e-readers are larger than the average handheld, giving you plenty of screen room. Better yet, hundreds of titles can be stored within your new library—a single microchip. (Please note that Ellora's Cave does not endorse any specific brands. You can check our website at www.ellorascave.com for customer recommendations we make available to new consumers.)

3. *Mobility.* Because your new library now consists of only a microchip, your entire cache of books can be taken with you wherever you go.
4. *Personal preferences are accounted for.* Are the words you are currently reading too small? Too large? Too...ANNOYING? Paperback books cannot be modified according to personal preferences, but e-books can.
5. *Innovation.* The way you read a book is not the only advancement the Information Age has gifted the literary community with. There is also the factor of what you can read. Ellora's Cave Publishing will be introducing a new line of interactive titles that are available in e-book format only.
6. *Instant gratification.* Is it the middle of the night and all the bookstores are closed? Are you tired of waiting days—sometimes weeks—for online and offline bookstores to ship the novels you bought? Ellora's Cave Publishing sells instantaneous downloads 24 hours a day, 7 days a week, 365 days a year. Our e-book delivery system is 100% automated, meaning your order is filled as soon as you pay for it.

Those are a few of the top reasons why electronic novels are displacing paperbacks for many an avid reader. As always, Ellora's Cave Publishing welcomes your questions and comments. We invite you to email us at service@ellorascave.com or write to us directly at: 1056 Home Avenue, Akron OH 44310-3502.